THE FORTUNES OF TEXAS

*Follow the lives and loves of a complex family
with a rich history and deep ties
in the Lone Star State*

HITTING THE JACKPOT

The Maloneys of Chatelaine, Texas,
have just discovered they are blood relations
to the Fortunes—which makes them instant
millionaires. But their inheritance comes
with a big secret attached that could change
everything for their small-town family...

When Linc Fortune Maloney goes from
rags to riches, he can't wait to start living large.
But his former coworker and longtime buddy
Remi Reynolds misses the old down-to-earth
Linc—the man she's been secretly crushing on
for years. And now Remi fears she's lost her
last chance to tell him how she really feels...

Dear Reader,

Happy New Year! I can't tell you how excited I get to start the new year—I love setting goals and creating new intentions, and I'm even more excited to celebrate by kicking things off with the first book in The Fortunes of Texas: Hitting the Jackpot series.

The question of what makes a person who they are was central to this story and one I had so much fun exploring. Everything about Lincoln Fortune Maloney's life changes thanks to an inheritance from Wendell Fortune, the grandfather he never knew. But Linc quickly discovers that fancy cars and lavish trips don't make him feel any different on the inside. He's still the same guy afraid of love and even more terrified of following in the footsteps of the father who left him and hurting the people he loves.

So when the person who captures his heart is his longtime friend Remi Reynolds, the one person he wants to protect, Linc has no idea how to handle things. For her part, Remi has loved Linc for years, so to have him suddenly want her by his side and in his bed is a bit overwhelming. But Remi wants something deeper than just a good time with Linc, and it's going to take a lot more than his bank account to impress her. Linc will have to risk everything if he's going to win Remi and make both of their dreams come true.

I hope you love reading Linc and Remi's story as much as I enjoyed writing it. Please reach out to me at michelle@michellemajor.com. I love hearing from readers!

Hugs,

Michelle

A Fortune's Windfall

MICHELLE MAJOR

HARLEQUIN
SPECIAL
EDITION

Special thanks and acknowledgment are given to
Michelle Major for her contribution to
The Fortunes of Texas: Hitting the Jackpot miniseries.

Recycling programs
for this product may
not exist in your area.

ISBN-13: 978-1-335-72437-3

A Fortune's Windfall

Copyright © 2022 by Harlequin Enterprises ULC

For questions and comments about the quality of this book,
please contact us at CustomerService@Harlequin.com.

Harlequin Enterprises ULC
22 Adelaide St. West, 41st Floor
Toronto, Ontario M5H 4E3, Canada
www.Harlequin.com

Printed in U.S.A.

Michelle Major grew up in Ohio but dreamed of living in the mountains. Soon after graduating with a degree in journalism, she pointed her car west and settled in Colorado. Her life and house are filled with one great husband, two beautiful kids, a few furry pets and several well-behaved reptiles. She's grateful to have found her passion writing stories with happy endings. Michelle loves to hear from her readers at michellemajor.com.

Books by Michelle Major

Harlequin Special Edition

Welcome to Starlight

The Best Intentions
The Last Man She Expected
His Secret Starlight Baby
Starlight and the Single Dad
A Starlight Summer
Starlight and the Christmas Dare

Maggie & Griffin

Falling for the Wrong Brother
Second Chance in Stonecreek
A Stonecreek Christmas Reunion

The Fortunes of Texas: The Wedding Gift

Their New Year's Beginning

The Fortunes of Texas: The Hotel Fortune

Her Texas New Year's Wish

The Fortunes of Texas: Rambling Rose

Fortune's Fresh Start

The Fortunes of Texas: Hitting the Jackpot

A Fortune's Windfall

Visit the Author Profile page
at Harlequin.com for more titles.

To the Fortunes of Texas team
of authors and editors. It's always a joy
to explore the world of the Fortunes with you.

Prologue

Lincoln Fortune Maloney turned in a circle in the small but well-tended backyard of his mother's modest house. The house that Linc, his three brothers and baby sister, Justine, had grown up in.

It had been cramped when they were kids. Almost unbearably so as he, Max, Cooper and Damon sprouted into gangly, long-limbed teenagers. He'd wished he could buy a bigger house for his mom and siblings. He was the man of the family, after all. At eight years old, Linc had been assigned that task by his father before Rick Maloney walked away and never looked back.

Now Linc was on the cusp of a new life. One that would change everything.

"Practicing your dance moves with those twirls?"

his youngest brother, Damon, asked with a laugh from the postage-stamp-sized patio.

"I'm thinking about what it will take to convince Mom to move to a nicer house." Linc shrugged. "If we actually receive the level of inheritance that old dude hinted at last month, I want to take care of her."

"We'll all take care of her," Damon, who at twenty-seven was five years younger than Linc, agreed, then wiggled his thick brows. "And have plenty left over to enjoy ourselves."

"I won't know where to start," Linc admitted as he ran a hand through his close-cropped, sandy-blond hair. He didn't consider himself frugal, but he was smart with the money he made. Hell, even his haircuts were cheap at the local barbershop he'd been going to since he was a boy.

"You better figure it out fast." Damon gestured him forward. "Justine and Stefan just arrived, and they brought Martin Smith with them. He wants to talk to you."

A bead of sweat rolled between Linc's shoulders that had nothing to do with the thick July air.

Chatelaine, Texas, was merely a speck on the map, oppressively hot in the way of most Lone Star towns in the summer months. But it was the place Linc had always called home.

A month ago, he'd traveled with his brothers and mom to Rambling Rose for his sister's wedding to Stefan Mendoza. Rambling Rose was another small dot on the map but one that was growing, thanks to the influx of new businesses and residents led by recently transplanted members of the well-known Fortune family.

Linc knew of the Fortunes—most people in Texas had heard of the influential family. In Chatelaine, it had been a branch of the Fortune family that had discovered and grown wealthy from one of the rich silver mines near town.

Linc didn't typically hobnob with people like the Fortunes. So at the wedding, he'd been shocked when it was revealed by Martin Smith that Linc and his siblings *were* Fortunes.

Unbeknownst to any of them, Rick Maloney had been the illegitimate son of Wendell Fortune, one of the brothers who'd operated the mine in Chatelaine.

It was still difficult for Linc to believe that his future in Chatelaine could be tied to the past. His hometown was nothing more than a tiny dot on the map, and he hadn't given much thought to something bigger. After all, the sign driving into town proudly advertised "Welcome to Chatelaine. The town that never changes. Harv's New BBQ straight ahead."

Linc ordered the pulled pork at Harv's every single visit.

Was it any wonder that thinking of how his life might change because of the inheritance made him question everything? He appreciated that Martin Smith was at least able to shed light on the father that had walked away from their family.

According to Martin, Rick had been declared

dead five years earlier after a motorcycle accident that had left him missing a year previous to that. But before Linc could process the loss of a father he barely remembered, Martin had explained that as the best friend of also deceased Wendell Fortune, he'd been tasked with tracking down Wendell's grandchildren and distributing the old man's considerable wealth among them.

Overnight, Linc had gone from nothing to being a Fortune with a potential fortune.

Potential because they hadn't heard anything from Martin since the wedding. Perhaps tonight Linc's promised future would change from potential to probable.

"This is it," he told his brother. "This is where everything changes."

Damon chucked him on the shoulder when Linc got to the patio. "You ready?"

"As I'll ever be."

They walked into the house, and Linc greeted his sister and new brother-in-law, then reached out his arms to take his baby nephew. Justine's son, Morgan, was now ten months old and had thankfully—as far as Linc could tell—helped to bridge the distance that had crept up in his sister's relationship with their mom.

Kimberly hadn't initially been supportive about Justine becoming a single mom. He knew his sister had been hurt by the perceived judgment and his mom regretted her actions.

He also believed that Kimberly's intentions had been pure. She'd been pregnant with Justine when her husband had walked away. His sister had never known anything but life with a single mom. She didn't realize how the abandonment affected Kimberly, but Linc knew.

He'd spent years supporting his mother and didn't bother to give credence to his own feelings about it. He'd locked them down tight the day his dad had pulled him aside in the front yard and told him to take care of his mom and siblings.

Rick never knew his daughter, and Linc's memories might be fuzzy, but he had more than any of his brothers did. He certainly understood how it felt to have a father involved in his life. For a short time, at least.

He turned and shook Martin Smith's hand.

"It's good to see you again, Lincoln," Martin said. "I guess you know why I'm here."

"Not just for my mom's excellent barbecue?" Linc answered.

"No." Martin took the glass of lemonade Kimberly handed to him. "I'd like to tell you…" He glanced around at the rest of the family. "All of you should hear this."

"Please have a seat," Linc said, gesturing to his mother's scuffed oak table. The chair scraped on the tile floor as Martin pulled it out and sat down.

"What do you know about your grandfather?" Martin asked after a long drink of the golden liquid.

Linc's stomach knotted as Max and Coop shared a confused look. Two years younger than Linc, Max was the most laid-back of the brothers. Since Max owned an accounting firm, Linc planned to ask him for advice on how to manage his new inheritance. He definitely wouldn't be asking advice from Coop. At twenty-nine, he was a consummate middle child, a bit of a wild troublemaker as a kid and always wanting the family spotlight on him.

Linc didn't like to think of his family being upset by a moment that should be a celebration. "Considering the fact that we only recently learned we even had a grandfather, there's not much we know."

"The Fortunes owned some sort of silver mine in Chatelaine back in the day," Kimberly said from where she stirred a pot of beans on the stove.

"Yes," Martin agreed. "Your grandfather Wendell and his brother, Walter, had several investment companies in town. A bank and the silver mine were the most prominent, but there was another mine… even more valuable."

"Another silver mine?" Cooper asked. "That's not exactly unique in this part of the state."

"A gold mine," Martin said slowly, seeming to take pleasure as each of the Maloney siblings reacted with great shock and excitement. "A secret gold mine, worth far more than any silver mine in the area."

Damon pumped his fist. "That's awesome. Go Grandpa Wendell."

"Exactly." Martin's beard twitched with amusement. He cleared his throat. "And since Rick Maloney is deceased…" He offered a sympathetic nod toward Kimberly. "I'm sorry to bring up a potentially difficult topic."

"It's fine," Linc's mom said, but Linc noticed her fingers tightened on the wooden spoon she still held.

In the days after Justine's wedding, Martin had explained that he'd hired an investigator to track down Rick, whom Linc and his family hadn't seen or heard from since he'd walked out on them when Kimberly was pregnant with Justine.

Martin had found Rick's second ex-wife, Roberta. According to Martin, Roberta had explained that Rick had left her after an argument six years ago and been traced to California, where it was believed he'd taken a curve too fast and driven his motorcycle off the highway and into the ocean.

"Yes, well…" Martin rubbed a hand along the back of his neck. "Since Rick is dead, his five children will inherit Wendell's estate."

"That's us." Damon nudged Max and Cooper, who stood on either side of him.

Justine smiled and bounced baby Morgan. "So what comes next, Martin?"

"Your grandfather had some specific stipulations, as I mentioned at the wedding." Martin grabbed a battered leather wallet out of his back pocket and stood to face Linc. "I have something for you, son."

Linc swallowed. He'd been prepared for this moment but now realized there was no way to truly be ready for what this meant in his life. For the lives of every member of his family. He had an idea about how much his grandfather's estate was worth.

At least he thought he had.

When Martin handed him the check, Linc's eyes grew wide and his stomach pitched. "Is this for real?"

"Yes, Lincoln. It's real."

His brothers gathered around, hooting and hollering over the number of zeros written on the check Martin had just given him.

"You'll all get an equal share of the estate," the man said with a nod. "Your grandfather had specific instructions as far as the timing for when and how the money will be distributed."

Linc was still trying to wrap his mind around what this check meant. He had more questions than answers at this point. "Thank you," he said. "Obviously none of us knew our grandfather."

"Some of us didn't even know our dad," Damon said. He'd been a toddler when Rick left and Linc knew he had no memories of the man who'd been his father.

"I can't change the past," Martin said, a note of remorse in his tone that Linc didn't quite understand.

In truth, this man had no responsibility toward them.

"I'm here now," Martin continued, "and I'm happy to give you this money, Lincoln. I'd tell you not to spend it all in one place, but I think that's a given."

Linc couldn't imagine spending in one lifetime the kind of money he'd just received. Since hearing about the inheritance at Justine's wedding, he'd thought about the fun he would have with it. He'd considered the places he wanted to travel and how he would take care of his mom and siblings.

That might not be everybody's version of fun, but Linc knew he would only be able to truly enjoy his new circumstances if he could also share it with the people he cared about.

Faced with the reality of how much things would be changing, he wasn't sure what to think. Would his new wealth lead to new responsibilities?

He'd lived a life of duty and commitment to his family because that was what was needed and expected. Although he planned on continuing to support them, he was also determined to enjoy his money and take a break from his obligations.

At least for a little while.

He didn't know how that would look quite yet, but it was his primary goal just the same.

"So what's first?" Max asked. "I mean, besides meeting with your very talented accountant brother to make sure all your ducks are in a row. We want to make sure your money works for you."

"That's the most boring thing I've ever heard," Cooper complained. "You should fly to Vegas. Do something crazy, *Indecent Proposal*-style."

Their mother clucked her disapproval. "I certainly hope Linc won't be following that advice."

"Not a chance," Linc assured her. Damon was the ladies' man in the family. Linc had only had one serious girlfriend in his life, and having his heart broken had been a harsh lesson that made it easy to remember why he didn't want to open himself up to that again.

"It might take some time," he said, "but I'll figure it out eventually."

"There's nothing wrong with taking time." Martin nodded in obvious approval. "Remember that you control this wealth, Lincoln. The money doesn't control you."

Linc wondered if his grandfather would have offered him the same advice. He glanced at the check again, then nodded and lifted his gaze to Martin's.

The old man smiled at him from beneath his bushy beard. "It will all work out."

"It will," Linc agreed. "And even though I never knew Wendell Fortune, I hope I can make him proud."

Chapter One

The Chatelaine Report: The biggest party this New Year's Eve won't be thrown by Fortune Metals or the Chatelaine Silver Company. An unknown host-with-the-most has rented out the LC Club on Lake Chatelaine for what's sure to be the most coveted invitation this town has seen in years. Everyone wants to know who the secret host is and how they can get on the guest list! Rumor has it that the master of ceremonies is a newcomer to Chatelaine's elite. One question remains on this inquiring mind: Why all the mystery?

"Girl, you can tug on that sexy dress all you want. The only thing you're going to do by covering your bottom half is reveal the assets the good Lord blessed you with on top."

Remi Reynolds's hand instinctively lifted to cover her chest as her coworker, Alana Searle, looked on, a mischievous twinkle in her blue eyes. "Seriously, Remi. You look amazing. Who knew you were hiding that spectacular figure under your sensible khaki pants and the purple apron only a giant stuffed dinosaur could appreciate?"

Remi had met Alana working at GreatStore, the only big-box franchise in their small town of Chatelaine. Remi loved her job in the book department at the busy store, although books hadn't been selling as well as they once did.

She also liked Alana, even though the two of them were opposites in almost every way. Alana was fun and vibrant, while Remi had no issues with her identity as a wallflower. There were plenty of examples in the novels she devoured in her free time of wallflowers who, by the end of the book, lived very happy lives. Remi didn't see why she had to be the exception to that rule.

Then Linc Maloney—now Lincoln *Fortune* Maloney—had invited most of the staff from GreatStore to a New Year's Eve bash at the LC Club on Lake Chatelaine, the only truly ritzy enclave in their small town.

On a whim, Remi had decided to uncover her previously nonexistent adventurous side. She'd borrowed a sparkly gold dress from her younger sister, Leah, and packed it to change into after her shift, since Linc had chartered a bus to pick up the party-goers in front of the store at closing.

In her haste that morning, Remi hadn't thought to try on the dress first or considered that Leah's figure was slenderer than her own. The dress, which hung loosely on her sister, hugged every one of Remi's curves. The plunging neckline revealed so much cleavage that she'd been half tempted to wear one of the purple GreatStore aprons Alana had referenced over the slinky sheath.

Her coworkers had exclaimed how great she looked to the point that Remi had gone beet red with embarrassment. Alec Ramsey and Paul Scott, Linc's two best friends on staff, had clearly seen how uncomfortable she was with the attention. They'd told her not to worry. Everyone knew she was still good old Remi, even if they suddenly realized she was a literal knockout.

Remi had appreciated both the compliment and the reassurance from her friends, but she couldn't stop fidgeting.

"Stop fidgeting," Alana told her. "We're almost there. This is going to be so fun. I can't believe Linc rented out the LC Club. On a store manager's salary he must have been saving for years. I've always wanted to be a guest at one of the swanky parties out here, haven't you?"

"I was a hostess at the LC Club back in high school." Remi tucked a lock of dark hair behind one ear, hoping Alana didn't notice her trembling hand.

"The place doesn't hold much appeal to me, although I'm excited to ring in the new year with my friends. Friends are important."

Alana gave her a distracted nod as they rolled down the tree-lined driveway that led to the club, with its impressive view of Lake Chatelaine behind the main building. "Especially friends who can spring for a place like this."

Remi didn't necessarily agree. She didn't care about money and knew it shouldn't make a person special or more important. She hoped Linc knew that, too. They'd been friends for the six years she'd worked a GreatStore, and although he was several years older than her, she also remembered him from high school.

He was serious and responsible, a terrific store manager, and a hard worker. Those were the qualities that impressed Remi, and Linc had them in spades. Maybe tonight, she would finally gather the courage to tell him how she felt—what was in her heart. In a town the size of Chatelaine, everyone knew the Maloney brothers. Remi had thought Linc was handsome back when she was a teenager. But when they'd started working together six years ago and she'd gotten to know him more…well…he'd been her unrequited crush for so long it was almost embarrassing. Tonight, she was already so out of her comfort zone in the dress that she might as well make the most of it.

From the moment the bus began to unload, it was

clear that her friends intended to make the most of the night. Staff in formal uniforms were ready to greet them with glasses of champagne. Based on the starstruck gazes of many of her coworkers, she knew she wasn't the only one who had never experienced something like this night.

The LC Club was a sprawling building with several balconies and terraces that offered a spectacular view of Lake Chatelaine. The architecture offered a mix of rustic flare and European elegance. She knew the stone used throughout had been mined in the southeastern part of the state and the exterior's neutral palette complimented the red slate roof tiles.

They entered the club and were shown to a ballroom with a full wall of windows that looked over the lake. The glass panels rose during the summer to invite in the lake breeze, but tonight the focus would be on the stone columns and archways through the reception area. A massive, curved granite bar was situated on the far side of the room next to the dance space with its honed teakwood floor.

Although darkness was quickly descending, twinkle lights lit the expansive patio behind the ballroom, and she could see a firepit glowing at the edge of the lake.

Swaths of gold and silver ribbon decorated the room. A bar had been set up at one end with tables displaying a variety of appetizers and desserts at the other.

There was a huge dance floor and a DJ, and each

of the round tables situated throughout the room had a candle centerpiece and fresh flowers.

Remi was still adjusting to the extravagance and obvious expense it took to make this party a reality when someone clinked a fork against a glass. A hush fell over the room. Everyone turned to where Linc stood on the DJ's platform, microphone in hand.

Like many men in attendance, he'd chosen a black tux for the occasion. Unlike anyone else, the way Linc wore his formal attire made Remi's pulse quicken and her knees go weak.

At a few inches over six feet, with sandy-blond hair, moss green eyes and an athletic build, Linc was handsome on a regular day. Tonight he looked every inch the wealthy big shot, a modern-day Jay Gatsby with his easy smile and dapper confidence.

She couldn't have taken her eyes off him if she tried. Thankfully, she didn't need to. Faint spots of pink bloomed high on his cheeks, and she wondered whether the color was due to excitement or if he'd started celebrating the coming new year early with the champagne he served the guests.

Remi had only taken a couple of sips but was already light-headed. The way she felt could be attributed to nerves, however, because tonight she was determined to tell Lincoln how she felt.

He cleared his throat, then began to speak, welcoming friends and family—she'd noted his three brothers in the room when the GreatStore staff had filed in.

"This night is not only a celebration of a new year," Linc told the crowd. "This is also the start of a new chapter in my life."

Someone—Remi was pretty sure it was Alec— bellowed, "Let's go" and the crowd cheered.

Linc's mouth curved at one corner, and he nodded. "That's what I plan to do," he announced, his smile growing. "Not many people outside my immediate family know this, but my siblings and I have inherited a literal fortune in addition to the Fortune name. Our grandfather, Wendell, whom we didn't know during his time here on earth, has left the five of us with an inheritance that can only be described as life-altering. Before I made any changes, I wanted to celebrate with the people who mean the most to me in life."

He scanned the room and winked at Alec and Paul before his gaze slid to Remi. If she wasn't mistaken, it took him a second to recognize her. His jaw appeared to go slack before he swallowed, Adam's apple bobbing.

"Right." He gave a slight shake of his head. "As I was saying, the new year will change a lot of things for me. One of which is my employment at GreatStore."

Remi's jaw fell open in shock. What was he talking about?

"As a few people on staff already know, I've handed in my resignation, effective at midnight. After nearly two decades working at GreatStore, it's time for me to move on to bigger and, hopefully, better things. I'm going to miss all of you."

"No." Remi wanted to scream her protest but hadn't realized she'd spoken the denial out loud until Alec clapped her on the shoulder.

"Oh yes. Only Paul and I knew about our boy's change of circumstance."

Paul laughed. "He's been sitting on that money for six months. It's about time he starts spending it and leaving us all behind."

"He's leaving?" Remi's voice shook.

"Not Chatelaine," Paul clarified. "Although who knows what greener pastures will eventually call to him. I just mean he's leaving the store. We'll miss him, that's for damn sure."

Alec leaned in as if he was sharing a secret. "Who knows? A man of Lincoln Fortune Maloney's means might need an entourage. I'll volunteer."

"Get in line," Paul told his friend with an elbow to the ribs. After a moment, the two men realized Remi wasn't laughing along with them.

"You okay?" Paul asked.

She forced a smile. "Maybe too much champagne."

"Pace yourself, lady," Alec commanded. "We have a long night of celebrating ahead of us."

"Got it," Remi promised as they walked away. In her heart, she knew there was nothing left for her to celebrate this night.

Linc wasn't sure he'd ever had his hand shaken or received so many hugs as he had this night. He hadn't been sure how his friends would react to the news of his inheritance.

Most of these people had known him for years, and he'd always been a simple guy. He supposed not much had changed inside him, although he certainly felt different. His brothers didn't understand why he'd sat on the money for so long without telling anyone about it.

He'd sworn them to secrecy, although he'd paid off his mother's house and his own. He'd tried to convince his mom to let him buy her something bigger, but she insisted she wanted to stay in the house where she'd raised her children—at least for now. Then he'd allocated a good chunk of the money to a financial advisor Max recommended. Other than that, he let the money sit in his account. He checked the balance every day, somehow not quite believing the fortune was his outright.

He kept expecting Martin Smith to show back up and tell Linc he'd made a horrible mistake or that someone was contesting the will. But the man not only hadn't come back to reclaim Linc's money, he also hadn't yet distributed anything to the rest of the Maloney siblings. Even so, Linc continued to be the only one with any doubt.

Finally at Christmas, his mother had pulled him aside and told him that she would support him however he chose to spend the money, but his anxiety and obsession over simply watching it wasn't healthy. He'd wanted to argue but knew she was right.

A few days after Christmas, when he'd decided to kick off his new life with this party, he'd told Alec and Paul about his change in circumstance. His friends had been excited but hadn't believed he could pull off the kind of New Year's blowout he wanted in such a short time.

Linc might not know much about being a millionaire, but he understood that he could make almost anything happen with the money at his disposal. And he had.

Earlier that night he'd slipped into the ballroom after taking a quick breather out front and had taken a moment to appreciate the sight. Most of the partygoers were on the dance floor or crowded around either the bar or the food tables. His friends and family were all in one place, laughing and dancing. He'd given this fun to them.

He wished his little sister could have joined them, but she and Stefan were in Rambling Rose. His mother had decided to stay home and watch the ball drop, her usual routine on New Year's Eve. Only tonight, she was watching on the brand new flat-screen television he'd bought her for Christmas.

A slight movement to his left caught Linc's attention. Remi Reynolds stood a few feet away on the other side of a potted palm. She hadn't noticed him come in as her eyes were trained on the dance floor, almost as if she were searching for someone.

Linc wondered who it could be and felt an unfamiliar stab of jealousy. But that was stupid. He and

Remi had been friends for years but nothing more. If she had a potential crush at the party, it was none of Linc's business.

He didn't understand why she wasn't mobbed with admirers. Remi was a naturally pretty woman on an average day. Tonight she looked almost unrecognizable in the tight-fitting, sparkly dress she wore. When he'd spotted her in the crowd, Linc's first thought had been that she looked like Wendell Fortune's golden treasure come to life.

A treasure he wanted to talk to, if nothing else.

"Are you having fun?" he asked as he moved around the plant into Remi's line of sight.

She looked up at him with those big hot-cocoa-colored eyes, and a flash of something in them that looked like yearning made his heart thump wildly against his rib cage.

Just as quickly, the flash was gone, replaced by her typical gentle amusement, but his heart didn't seem to get the message. He rubbed two fingers against his chest as though he could physically calm the sensation. Until this moment, Linc hadn't felt like he'd overindulged, but maybe he'd had one too many glasses of champagne.

"It's a lovely evening," Remi said. "Thank you for including me."

"Of course you're included, Rem. We're friends."

Her brow puckered at his words, and he was unsure whether he'd added the reminder of their friendship for her sake or his.

"Congratulations on your inheritance. It must be exciting."

"Overwhelming," he admitted. "But I'm getting used to it."

"I'm— Everyone is going to miss you at Great-Store."

Was it his imagination, or did her smile seem forced? "Chatelaine is a small town. It's not like I'm moving away."

"It won't be the same," she said quietly, then lifted a hand to fiddle with the gold hoop in one ear.

The music changed to a popular dance tune, and Remi glanced toward the crowd again.

"We should dance," he said, holding out a hand.

She stared at it like he was offering her a poisonous snake. "I'm not much of a dancer, more a watcher."

"Tonight is different," he told her, crooking a finger. "Special."

She bit down on her glossy lower lip, and Linc once again reminded himself that he and Remi were just friends. She was not his type. Ever since his high school girlfriend had broken up with him for not being upwardly mobile enough, Linc had made sure to date women who weren't interested in his prospects or in any sort of serious attachment.

He liked to have fun, but he knew the consequences of expectations and wanting too much or giving more of his heart than was safe. Remi was the kind of woman who deserved a man who could fully commit, and Linc didn't have it in him to be that guy.

Friendship was safer, although now that he'd suggested the dance, he couldn't imagine anything he wanted more than pulling her into his arms, even for a few minutes. The idea of being attracted to Remi was so new and unexpected, it made his chest buzz like he'd just taken a hit of caffeine. It had to be the dress and the excitement of the evening.

There was no way it could be anything more.

"Special," she repeated and almost hesitantly placed her hand in his.

Her fingers were warm, and her hand fit with his like it was meant to be there. He didn't believe in destiny, but there was no denying his heart settled like a puzzle piece falling into place as he led Remi to the dance floor.

They made their way to the center of the crowd. She grinned self-consciously as he twirled her. The light from the chandelier in the center of the room reflected off her gold dress and made it look like she was glowing.

A moment later, the song changed to a slow ballad. Remi's eyes widened, but before either of them could overthink things, he pulled her close.

He'd danced with several coworkers already tonight. This was no different.

Even though it felt different. Special.

If Linc had been aware of how well their hands fit together, having Remi's curves pressed against his body was a revelation. Those curves were mostly hidden by her GreatStore apron or the casual clothes she favored around town, but now his body was ridiculously attuned to hers.

Definitely too much champagne, he told himself. It took two stanzas of the song before she finally relaxed against him, and he smiled as she rested her cheek against his shoulder. It was one dance, the same as all the others. It didn't mean anything.

He looked around the ballroom at the other couples on the dance floor, then at Alec and Paul, who stood near the bar with a few people from the store's outdoor section. These were his friends. This was the life he'd known,

Linc had gotten a job at GreatStore on his fifteenth birthday, first in the stockroom and then working in various departments on the floor. It was important to him to be able to help his mom financially, and he didn't mind the long days. He liked being busy and knowing he was pulling his weight as the de facto man of the house.

When he'd returned to Chatelaine after leaving college, one of his former bosses had made him assistant manager of the lawn and garden department. He'd liked the job well enough. Customer service suited his personality, and he enjoyed the fact that every day offered different challenges. Being a full-time college student felt almost too indulgent for Linc.

He did miss the social side of college, so meeting

Paul and Alec, who were both working in the stock-room at the time, had been an added bonus.

The three of them got along great from the start, and both were promoted to assistant manager at the same time he was named manager of electronics.

His life wasn't exciting by most people's standards, but it worked for him. He hadn't expected anything more, but he was getting more in spades thanks to his late grandfather and Martin Smith.

Of course, he felt sentimental with Remi. In a lot of ways, she represented his life. His old life. The one that was changing on every level. Even if he wanted more, now wasn't the time.

Linc had never had a choice about the man he needed to become. That had been taken away the day his father walked out of their lives. Thanks to his inheritance, now he could do anything—be anything. Although change was hard, he wouldn't let it derail him from making the most of this new life.

He couldn't get sidetracked by how Remi felt in his arms or how much he would miss his friends at the store. He needed to embrace change and action. To leap into whatever adventures his new life as a wealthy man would bring his way.

So, even though his arms seemed to ache with the desire to hold onto her, Linc released Remi when the music stopped. The DJ announced the countdown to midnight as the crowd cheered. A moment later, Paul and Alec joined them on the dance floor.

The energy of the room was palpable and intoxicating. Although it felt like ripping away a part of himself, Linc made sure to position his two friends between him and Remi.

His body's reaction was one thing, but he was in control. He knew the strange connection simmering between them tonight was a result of champagne bubbles, a sparkly dress, and nothing more.

As the DJ announced the official start of the new year, the crowd went wild. Linc man-hugged Paul and Alec, and then gave Remi a quick hug. It would have been wrong if he'd brushed her aside at this point. They were friends. It didn't need to mean anything.

He pulled back, planning to move on to the next person waiting to wish him a happy new year, but Remi held on for a moment.

Her eyes were luminous as her gaze collided with his. He wasn't sure if she was aware of licking her lips, but his body clenched in response to the gesture.

"Happy New Year," she said, her voice breathless.

For a moment, Linc felt as though she were going to reach up on tiptoe and kiss him. Then Paul grabbed her by the shoulders and spun her away.

"Happy New Year, Rem." Paul hitched a thumb toward Linc. "We're going to survive without this guy. You wait and see."

She looked over her shoulder at Linc, and he got the impression she wanted to protest, but someone clapped him on the back and he turned away. It was just as well.

It was better for both of them this way.

Chapter Two

"That party was epic." The following morning, Alana bounced into the staff lounge and opened her locker with so much force that the door banged into the next locker.

Remi winced at the sound of metal against metal. "About as epic as my headache," she said with a groan. "I didn't even drink that much."

"Which is more than you usually drink," Alana pointed out. "I saw you dancing just before midnight. Be honest, is that the latest you've ever stayed up? Definitely past your bedtime."

"So funny," Remi muttered as she grabbed a bottle of pain reliever from her locker. She wasn't about to admit that Alana was right. No sense in advertising how pathetically small her life was.

The saddest part was that she hadn't considered

herself or her life pathetic before last night, even though plenty of her coworkers would. She didn't care about her lack of social life, except hearing Linc talk about exciting new adventures confirmed what she'd already suspected.

She was too dull for him to consider as anything other than a friend. Honestly, if she heard him describe their relationship in terms of being friends one more time, she felt like she would scream.

Downing a couple of pills with a big swig of water to get her pounding head under control, she turned to find Alana grinning at her.

"What?" she demanded. "Why do you look so chipper this morning? Do you have some kind of hangover cure that I need to learn?"

Alana shook her head, bright blond waves bouncing around her shoulders. "I'm not hungover."

"How is that possible?" Remi shut her locker's metal door as quietly as she could manage. "I figured everyone at the party would be feeling the effects today."

"I didn't drink." Alana looked wickedly proud of herself, then shrugged when Remi snorted. "It's true."

"Why not?"

Her bubbly coworker frowned slightly. "No specific reason. I'm taking a break and cleaning out my system. You know what I mean. New year, new intentions."

"Right. Well, I'm starting with the intention never to feel like this again."

Alana had no way of knowing that Remi was talking about more than simply a headache due to too much champagne. The heartache at Remi's missed opportunity with Linc would take more than a greasy breakfast and a couple of ibuprofen to eliminate.

The slow dance they'd shared had been magic, and that wasn't the alcohol talking. Molding herself to Linc's hard body while they swayed on the dance floor felt like every one of Remi's fantasies come to life. His arms around her had been strong and sure, and the heat radiating from him had elicited an answering pull of warmth in her.

They'd been friends for years, and it was only mildly humiliating to admit—even to herself—that for years she'd been gathering tiny bits of information about him, like a magpie hoarding shiny objects. She knew his preferences in food, how he took his coffee, the scent of his shampoo, and that he favored fruit-flavored chewing gum. So many little details collected, but in six years of friendship, she hadn't known what it felt like to be in his arms.

Until last night, when it was too late. The realization that it was more perfect than she could have imagined didn't do her any good now.

She'd promised herself that she would be brave, but in the brief moment when she could have kissed him, she'd hesitated. Then the moment was over.

Linc was moving on to bigger and better things, and Remi would just be someone from his past. She gripped the front of her apron after tying it tightly, as if she could squeeze out her sadness at losing something she never really had.   .

"How rich do you think Linc is?" Alana asked, her voice hushed. "I wonder if he's going to need someone to help him spend all that money. I'm an excellent shopper and an even better traveling companion. I might volunteer for the position."

Remi'd been amused at Alex's entourage comment last night, but Alana's words felt like a sucker punch to the gut. As far as Remi knew, Linc and Alana had never been an item, but the beautiful, fun-loving blonde was precisely the kind of woman he might choose.

Not someone like Remi, whose idea of fun was a night of puzzles—she loved puzzles—and a movie marathon. Or hours spent curled on her mother's sofa with a favorite book and endless cups of chamomile tea. That was Remi's idea of heaven. She could already imagine losing herself in the pages of a book after her shift ended, the only surefire way she knew to forget her troubles.

"How would you spend the money if you got an inheritance like Linc's?"

"I have no idea," Remi answered. She couldn't imagine her life changing in that way, and still wondered how Linc was processing it. They'd been friends long enough that she felt like she knew him, and she guessed his change in financial status was a huge adjustment.

"Come on, Rem. You could buy a fancy car or

splurge on a whole new wardrobe. Book the trip of a lifetime. Everyone has a dream trip in mind. Where would you go if you could take a lavish vacation?"

Alana's eyes sparkled as she and Remi exited the lounge on the way to their respective departments.

"Anywhere?" Remi's mind drifted to her favorite books as she processed Alana's question. "Hogwarts," she answered without thinking. "Or maybe Narnia."

At Alana's loud chuckle, she blinked. "What are you talking about?" her friend asked with a shake of her head. "I know you're supersmart and all. Is Narnia some private island getaway I don't know about?"

"No, it's…" Remi wasn't sure how much to reveal to Alana. Most of her coworkers teased her about her propensity for reading.

She almost always had a book in her locker and often spent her lunch hour reading, especially if Linc wasn't around. Her heart stung after his announcement about resigning from GreatStore last night. He was one of the few people who didn't seem to care that she was a bookworm.

It felt silly to admit that she'd been planning her night around rereading one of her favorite book series. Sometimes it felt like the characters in the novels she loved were just as real as any living, breathing person.

"What's so funny?" a familiar voice asked behind her.

She whirled to see Lincoln standing at the edge of the kitchen accessory aisle. He inclined his head as his gaze moved from her to Alana. *Use your words, Remi*, she commanded herself but seemed unable to put together one coherent sentence.

"Remi and I were just talking about what trip we'd take first if we won the lottery or found out we had a rich relative who left us a fortune."

Linc massaged a hand over the back of his neck as he stepped toward them, appearing vaguely uncomfortable at the reminder of his inheritance. He wore a white button-down and dark jeans, much as he used to when he worked at GreatStore, although he no longer needed to accessorize with a purple apron. "I haven't planned a vacation, but it's not a bad idea. Do you have any suggestions for me?"

Alana's laugh turned throaty. "I suggest that you make me your travel companion," she told Linc. "I'd choose someplace like Paris or Hawaii. Remi wants to go to Hogworld."

"Hogwarts," Remi mumbled as her cheeks grew hot.

Alana nudged her. "Apparently, she has some farmer vacation fantasies."

The store's PA system crackled, and Alana was paged to customer service. "Keep me in mind if you want to brainstorm tropical vacation ideas," she called to Linc as she moved away.

Remi fiddled with the edge of her purple apron. "I don't have farming fantasies."

"I wouldn't judge you if you did," Linc said with a gentle smile. "Also, if I could find a way to platform nine and three-quarters, I'd invite you to go with me."

It felt like sparkles bursting over her head as she looked into his amused gaze. He not only wasn't making fun of her, but he'd understood the reference without her having to explain it.

Was it any wonder she thought he was perfect?

"In that case, the butterbeer would be my treat." Linc grinned. "Wouldn't that be something?"

Anything with him would be something, but Remi reminded herself that last night had changed everything between them, only not the way she wanted. In fact...

"What are you doing here?" She glanced around, surprised when neither Paul nor Alec materialized from one of the aisles. She might have expected Linc to be at the store visiting one of his friends, but he seemed to be on his own.

He flashed a sheepish smile. "Geez, Remi. You know how to make a guy feel welcome."

"I'm happy to see you," she said quietly, embarrassment ricocheting through her. "But I thought you quit GreatStore?"

"I needed a few things..." He gestured to the kitchen aisle. "A new coffee maker for one. I worked so many opening shifts that I didn't bother replacing mine when it went on the fritz a few months ago."

Remi laughed. "Alana dreams of a shopping trip that involves a fancy car and new wardrobe. You start with a coffee maker. That's what I like about you, Linc. You're practical."

She meant the words as a compliment but could tell he didn't take them that way when his brows drew together.

"Actually…" He shoved his hands into his pockets and rocked back on his heels.

Linc's thinking stance, Remi mused. She'd seen him make the same movement dozens of times before, in staff meetings or when he was pondering a big idea.

"You know what? I *am* going to buy a new car. Today."

"Oh."

"How exciting," Alana said as she popped out of a nearby aisle. "I hope it's something fast and flashy."

She mimicked steering a car and made a few growly engine noises before dissolving into laughter. "You can turn Chatelaine on its ear."

"Definitely," he agreed and shot a glance toward Remi. "It would be nice to have a friend with me to help make the ultimate decision."

"I volunteer," Alana shouted, waving her arm like she was trying to entice a teacher to call on her. "But you have to let me drive. I promise not to hit speeds over two digits." She winked at Linc. "Not for long, anyway."

"Well…that's a nice offer." Linc looked distinctly uncomfortable. "I was actually thinking of taking Remi. It would help to have someone practical along to keep me from going too wild."

Remi blinked. A part of her loved that Linc would choose her to accompany him for his first big purchase, but her enthusiasm was tempered, knowing he wanted her because she'd be perfect in the role of wet blanket.

When Linc looked at Remi, her silly heart wanted to melt. "What do you say?" he asked with a half-smile. "Are you up for an adventure?"

Alana sniffed. "Remi doesn't do adventure. You have to tell her it's an assignment. She's good at assignments."

Remi wanted to argue, but Alana was right. Linc was good at assignments, too. Until last night, she hadn't even known he yearned for adventure.

"An adventurous assignment," he amended.

"Could one of you help me find something called a mandolin?" The three of them turned to where a customer stood, a bewildered expression on his face. "My mom wants one for her birthday. I thought it was a musical instrument."

The customer was an attractive man who looked to be in his late twenties, probably from out of town, because Remi hadn't seen him around before today.

Alana's eyes lit up. "I can help you," she told him. "It's so sweet that you're shopping for your mama." She led him down the kitchen aisle, leaving Linc and Remi on their own.

Linc lifted one thick brow as he studied Remi, and she realized he was waiting for her answer. "I work today," she said.

"Right." His mouth pulled down at the corners, and she liked the idea that he was disappointed. Maybe he really did want to take her along, as opposed to Paul or Alec.

"I'm off tomorrow," she blurted. "We could go then?"

He rewarded her with a wide grin. "I'll pick you up at nine thirty."

"Okay." She wasn't sure what else to say but didn't want this moment—any moment with Linc—to end.

"I should get back to the book department," she said finally. "We got a new shipment of healthy cookbooks in. All the rage in the new year."

"And I should..." Linc threw up his hands like he wasn't sure what he should be doing.

"You should go pick out your coffee maker," she reminded him.

"Yeah." He flashed her another grin. "I'll see you tomorrow, Remi."

It was a good thing Remi had needed to wait a day for the car-buying road trip, Linc thought as they headed toward San Antonio the following morning. They were traveling north for the two-hour trip to a bigger city since Chatelaine was far too small for the type of car dealerships Linc wanted to visit.

Until the conversation with her and Alana, buying a car hadn't been on his to-do list. His current problem was that he didn't have a to-do list.

Linc had been working at GreatStore since he

turned fifteen. At thirty-three, that was over half his life. And even before he'd been old enough for a part-time job, he'd had more than his share of responsibility with helping take care of his younger siblings.

He had no idea where to start when he had nothing to do.

Buying a new coffeepot, a rice cooker and a new set of steak knives had at least given him a purpose for a few minutes, plus a bit of an adrenaline rush, if he was being honest. It was still strange to walk into a store—even one as basic as GreatStore—and realize he didn't have to adhere to a strict budget for the first time in his life.

As the store manager, he'd made a decent salary with excellent benefits, but Linc had continued to support his mom and save as much as he could, so he lived frugally.

But not anymore.

He glanced over at Remi, who was gazing out the window of his practical—and boring—base model truck with a smile playing around the corners of her mouth.

She seemed thrilled to be joining him today and had started the drive to San Antonio talking a mile a minute, more than he'd ever heard her speak at one time. Her enthusiasm about topics ranging from professional sports to obscure poetry charmed him, plus she made him feel relaxed when nerves about what it meant to live like a multimillionaire threatened to take over.

For a woman who wasn't known for her sense of adventure, she certainly seemed delighted to be on this one with him.

Eventually, they'd settled into a comfortable silence, although he couldn't help wondering what was going on in her brain at the moment.

"German or Italian?" he asked as they began to pass billboards that announced they were getting closer to the city.

She gave him a quizzical look. "For lunch?"

"For a car," he clarified with a laugh. "That's the whole purpose of why we're here today."

A blush stained her cheeks. "I haven't given either type much thought." She tapped an elegant finger on her chin. "I guess I'd vote German."

"German it is."

"Linc, no," she exclaimed. "You can't decide on the make of a car based on my opinion. It's your money."

He shrugged. "I have plenty of it. If I wanted to, I could drive one of each. A whole fleet of cars."

"You don't need a whole fleet," she said with an adorable eye roll.

"Needing and wanting are two different things."

Her smile faded. "Yes, I know."

Before he could decipher what she meant, Remi sat up straighter and pointed out the front window at the dealership ahead. "Look at all of these posh cars. This is quite a departure from the used car lot in Chatelaine where I bought my hatchback."

"This baby is from that same lot." Linc patted his dashboard. "But I'm trading up today."

He pulled into the ritzy dealership and parked near the sales office. "Let's go spend some money," he told Remi.

She looked uncomfortable with the thought of that but followed him across the lot when no one came to greet them.

"Silver or black?" he asked as he walked between two equally sleek models.

"Silver."

"That was definitive."

"Black will get too hot in the summer. It's a practical consideration."

He grinned. They were standing among cars so expensive, some of them cost more than he'd made in a year at GreatStore, and Remi was thinking about practicality.

"Hey, there. Can I help y'all with something?"

Linc turned to see a man only a few years older than him striding toward them. The sales guy wore a gray button-down and similarly hued tie with charcoal-colored pants. Linc had on jeans and a sweatshirt, his typical day off uniform. Although now every day was off, so he might need to rethink his wardrobe.

"I'd like to buy a car," Linc said. The salesman, whose name tag read Greg, gave him a subtle once-over if he wasn't mistaken.

"We've got some real beauties in stock today."

He gestured toward the back of the lot. "Our entry-level sedans offer a perfect combination of comfort and class at an affordable price point. If you want to follow me—"

"I don't." Linc crossed his arms over his chest. "I'm looking for something more luxurious."

"Sure," Greg agreed with an unmistakably patronizing smile. "Is that your truck parked in front of the sales office?"

Remi moved closer to Linc, like she wanted to put herself between him and the rude sales guy.

"It is."

"We can't give you more than blue book value for the trade-in on it."

"Not a problem. What's your top-of-the-line model?"

Greg scoffed out a laugh. "As I said, I can show you some great options if you'll follow me."

"Entry-level options," Linc repeated. He was beginning to feel more than irritated with the man's attitude. Linc had worked with customers on all budget levels during his years at GreatStore, and he'd never made anyone feel like less.

"A big step-up from what you're used to," Greg countered.

"How do you know what he's used to?" Remi demanded.

Linc glanced down at her, surprised to see her fists clenched and color high in her cheeks. Remi rarely got mad, as far as he knew. He'd seen her deal with even the most annoying, irate customer with a generous amount of deference. But now she looked ready to pummel Greg and his too-many-shades-of-gray ensemble.

"It's fine, Remi." He placed a hand on her arm and squeezed. "We've seen enough here anyway."

"I'm not trying to chase you away," Greg said, his tone slipping into a heavy Texas drawl. "We've got plenty of awesome vehicles for you to check out."

"No, thanks," Linc answered as he steered Remi back to his truck. She didn't argue and obviously knew where they were headed, but he kept his hand on the small of her back.

It felt right, like she was both grounding him and giving him strength.

"But I gotta tell you something, Gregory," he said over his shoulder, easily matching the man's twang, "you're making a big mistake here. Huge."

He heard Remi's stifled laugh at his movie reference and felt a grin spread across his face. This was the effect she had on him. Moments earlier, he was practically grinding his teeth to dust with annoyance. Now he just wanted to laugh at the whole situation.

Linc didn't need a random sales guy to confirm his self-worth. He knew what he could afford, even if the world didn't realize his changed circumstances.

As important as knowing himself, he knew the woman at his side. Somehow, Linc understood there was nothing he couldn't handle while Remi was with him.

The feeling both terrified and exhilarated him, a

sensation that was becoming typical the more time he spent with her.

And he didn't want it to end.

Chapter Three

Twenty minutes later, Remi slipped into the passenger seat of a shiny red Ferrari and fastened her seat belt as Linc adjusted the driver's seat to accommodate his long legs.

Things had been tense when they'd pulled out of the previous dealership, and she'd wondered if the rude sales guy had ruined their day with his attitude. But less than ten minutes down the road, Linc had pulled into the Ferrari dealership. They'd no sooner parked in front of the sleek showroom with its wall of windows that a salesman in a tailored suit had approached the car.

Remi'd wanted to cringe, worried that they might receive the same reception as at the previous dealership. But when Linc told Bill, the older man with dark hair and hawkish nose, that he was interested in buying a car on the spot, they'd been treated like royalty.

Since Linc would be the one test driving the car, he'd been given a tall glass of water while Remi was offered a crystal flute of champagne.

The man had explained that in order to be eligible to buy a brand new Ferrari, Linc would have to establish a relationship with the dealership by purchasing one of the pre-owned models available on the lot. But he was respectful and gracious as he detailed the purchase process for the Italian auto, which he described as 'a racing car for the street.'

Linc had visibly relaxed and the two men had struck up quite a rapport as they discussed the different models and the history of the luxury product and the company's late founder, Enzo Ferrari.

Even Remi, who didn't know the first thing about cars or care one whit for speed or horsepower, was excited by the prospect of riding in one of the distinctive sports cars.

She was even more impressed by the purring of the engine as Linc drove out of the lot and the way the car vibrated on the road along with the feel of the luxurious leather seat.

"I think I'm becoming a fan of fast cars," she said with a laugh.

Linc grinned at her then turned his gaze back to the road. "Let's see what this baby can do," he murmured as he took the on-ramp to the interstate.

After checking to make sure the lane was clear, he punched the gas pedal.

Remi's breath caught in her throat as the car accelerated, wickedly fast but smooth like silk.

"Slow down," she told him suddenly, reaching out to place her hand on his arm.

With a questioning glance, Linc eased off the gas. "What's wrong?"

"My heart is going to beat out of my chest," she told him. "I'm sorry. Maybe I was the wrong person to come along with you."

"You are exactly the right person," he said as he signaled and changed lanes. "You didn't even flinch when I did my pathetic Pretty Woman routine at the first dealership."

"I liked it. I liked that you stood up for yourself, but I'm glad you didn't give up." She smoothed a hand over the dark dash. "This car is so luxurious. It's a good fit for you."

"I'm not sure about that, but I'm buying it." He checked the rearview mirror. "I just wish I could really let loose and see what it can do."

"I'm happy going the speed limit." She wondered if the admission would make her seem boring.

"I'm happy if you're happy," he said with a smile then took the next exit. They headed back in the direction of the Ferrari showroom but had to pass the first dealership on the way.

Remi pointed and then clapped her hands together. "You have to pull in. I know you have more Julia Roberts in you."

Linc laughed again, and he looked so carefree. She rarely saw him that way, and it made her heart happy to think he could relax so much with her. "I don't want to be a jerk."

"*You* aren't the jerk," she reminded him.

"What the hell," he muttered and maneuvered into the lot with enough speed to make Remi gasp.

He hit the brakes hard and the car came to a sudden and yet not jarring stop.

Within seconds, the salesman from earlier moved toward them from a nearby row of cars.

"May I help you?" he asked with far more friendliness than he'd shown earlier.

Linc rolled down the window and waved. "Do you remember me?"

The man's jaw went slack as he nodded.

"I said you were making a big mistake. Huge, in fact. Pro tip from one customer service professional to another—don't judge a book by its cover, man, or you could wind up losing out on the sale of a lifetime. You understand?"

"Yeah," the sales guy said through gritted teeth. "Great car, by the way."

"I know," Linc said then hitched a thumb at Remi. "Turns out red is her favorite color."

Then he hit the button to roll up the window and sped out of the lot. "Too melodramatic?" he asked with a wink as he neared the Ferrari dealership.

"I thought it was perfect," she answered. "This whole day has been perfect. I don't want it to end."

"How about lunch? After I finish the paperwork on my new ride, we could grab something before heading back to Chatelaine. Unless you have plans and need to get home."

"No plans," she said, proud her voice didn't shake. The thought of spending more time with Linc made her tingle from head to toe.

He pulled back into the lot, where Bill was waiting. Remi occupied herself by watching a daytime talk show in the showroom's opulent lounge while Linc completed the sale. By the time they left, the dealership's manager had outfitted them both with an array of Ferrari merchandise from ball caps to perfume to custom sunglasses.

"Where are we going?" she asked as they drove out of the lot a half hour later in Linc's gorgeous new car.

"Bill made a reservation for us." His grin grew playful. "It's a surprise."

Remi had never liked surprises, but as with everything involving Linc, it felt different when he was in control.

The downtown San Antonio skyline came into view, and soon after, Linc pulled into the valet entrance at an opulently appointed boutique hotel.

Remi's heart pounded in her chest. "What are we doing here?"

"Lunch," he answered like it was no big deal. "I

once had a customer at the store, a family spending the summer on the lake. The guy must have bought half the sporting goods department. He asked me where to get a good burger in town and told me that the best burger he'd ever had was at the restaurant at this hotel. I don't know why it stuck with me. Right now, it seems like the pinnacle of luxury to be able to afford a five-star hamburger, so we're going to try it. Are you up for a culinary adventure?"

Remi wasn't sure how to answer, but her first instinct was to steer him toward something more practical. She was certain they could find a perfectly adequate burger at a much cheaper place.

Then she took in Linc's expression and saw how excited he seemed about the prospect of experiencing what he considered a wealthy man's lunch. The decision was taken out of her hands a moment later when the valet opened her door.

As Remi exited the car, she heard the valet taking the keys from Linc, exclaiming over the vehicle and its features.

Even someone like her, with no knowledge of cars, understood that the Ferrari was something special. Yet hearing the way the men surrounding Linc discussed it proved that even more.

She was happy for her friend, but it also made her realize that if he were behind the wheel of such a remarkable car, pretty soon he would want a special woman in the seat next to him. Remi wouldn't kid herself into believing she was that kind of woman.

Linc winked as he came around the front of the car and placed a hand on her shoulder.

"I feel like James Bond," he said against her ear as they entered the swanky but understated hotel.

"I can see why that comparison appeals more than Julia Roberts," Remi answered with a breathless laugh. Lincoln Fortune Maloney had his arm around her. Maybe it was a good thing he was grounding her. Otherwise, she might float away on a cloud of happiness.

"That makes you a Bond girl," he said and released her after a playful tug on her hair.

With that comment, Remi came crashing down to earth. There was no way anyone would mistake her for a Bond girl, even one of the most understated examples. She'd be more the brainy sidekick of the hero as opposed to the love interest.

She didn't bother explaining that to Linc. Clearly, he was just being kind anyway.

The hostess sat them at a table near the window with a picture-perfect view of the downtown river walk. Remi felt almost nervous as Linc immediately ordered several appetizers and a bottle of sparkling water.

"That's a lot of food," she said, smoothing the crisp white napkin over her lap. "You might not need the burger."

"I heard your stomach growling at the dealership," Linc told her. "I figured I should feed you properly."

"I had a granola bar in my purse," she said quietly, then gasped as she looked at the lunch selections. "Linc, the hamburger is twenty-eight dollars. Do they put diamonds in the ketchup at this place?"

He chuckled. "Remi, order two burgers if you want them. It's all good. I can afford it."

She frowned and tried to think about how to ask him what she wanted to know. "Are you sure? Do you ever worry there's been a mistake? What if you don't have as much disposable income as you think?"

"I have more than you could imagine." He placed his palms on the tablecloth and leaned forward. "I've had my inheritance for over six months, so I'm confident no one will come after me. It's not a mistake."

"Six months?" Her mouth dropped open, and she snapped it closed, then thanked the waiter who poured her a glass of sparkling water. Bubbles exploded on the surface, and Remi silently marveled at the idea of paying for water in a restaurant when they could give it to customers free from the tap. "You've been wealthy for six months?" she asked him once they were alone again.

He nodded, then took a long drink. The next thing Remi knew, Linc was coughing up a storm. "The fizz went up my nose."

She giggled and wagged a finger at him. "That doesn't happen with free, flat water."

"Worth it," he said as he cleared his throat.

The waiter brought the appetizers Linc had ordered, calamari and bruschetta, and took their lunch orders. Remi chose a spinach salad while Linc ordered a cheeseburger with sweet potato fries.

"I've never had calamari," Remi admitted as she studied the breaded bites that looked like mini onion rings.

"Me, neither," Linc flashed a conspiratorial smile. "We'll have our first time together."

"Oh."

His eyes widened as if he'd just realized the innuendo in his statement.

Remi quickly plucked up a calamari ring, dipped it in sauce and shoved it into her mouth. "Mmm…"

She pointed to the basket of calamari and then to Linc. He grabbed a piece and ate it, not even bothering with sauce.

"Calamari virgins no more," she said before thinking better of it.

They burst into fits of laughter and reminded Remi that regardless of his money or her awkwardness or whatever the future might bring, she and Linc were friends. She enjoyed hanging out with him, a feeling that had grown over the course of the day.

A tiny part of her had wondered if they'd have anything to talk about outside of GreatStore, but it was easy to share stories of her childhood and listen to his tales of helping to raise his four younger siblings.

She knew Linc was a stand-up guy who still helped take care of his mother. He'd also played a big part in guiding his three brothers and Justine when they were younger. Although his sister had moved away, Max, Cooper and Damon still lived in Chatelaine, and each of them came into the store on occasion.

The camaraderie between the brothers was obvious and infectious. Being around them lightened Linc's usually serious disposition.

The inheritance seemed to be having that same effect, as she'd never seen him laugh as much as he did today. It would be nice to believe that she had something to do with his high spirits, but Remi didn't give herself that much credit.

Their food arrived, and she couldn't resist when he offered her a bite of his burger. It was, indeed, the best hamburger she'd ever had, although part of her enjoyment had to do with sharing it with Linc.

Although they were both stuffed, he insisted on ordering every dessert on the menu, citing Remi's well-known sweet tooth as grounds for indulging.

She only put up a half-hearted argument. She'd ordered a salad for lunch, after all. Besides, the selections were too difficult to resist—from the salted caramel crème brûlée to a perfectly executed flourless chocolate cake to a tangy key lime pie. Even the sorbet selection was superb, reminding her of eating raspberries on a hot summer day.

"My dad would have loved this," she told Linc as a spoonful of the fresh, icy goodness melted on her tongue. "Raspberry was his favorite flavor."

"You miss him a lot." Linc made the words a statement instead of a question, so she didn't bother to deny it.

"Sometimes it's hard to believe he's gone. It's been over six years, but I swear there are nights when I still expect him to walk through the back door and make some comment about my mom being the best cook in the history of the world. She loved making food for him because it made him so happy."

"He was a good dad." Another statement rather than a question.

"The best," Remi confirmed anyway.

"That must have been nice."

The waiter brought the check at that moment, distracting Linc for a few seconds as he pulled out his wallet and dug out some cash. Remi was grateful because there'd been so much yearning in his voice when he spoke of her father—a deep wistfulness she doubted he even noticed. She needed a moment to collect her emotions before meeting his gaze again.

"I was lucky in that way." She pushed back from the table as the waiter walked away. "Even with three girls, our house was strangely quiet, and I often wished for more excitement. You must have had an abundance."

He laughed as he pocketed his wallet. "Excitement and chaos aren't the same thing. You wanted noise. All I wanted was peace and quiet." A panicked look crossed his face.

"What?"

"Nothing." He shook his head. "I just reminded

myself of something I would never want to emulate." He stopped in the middle of the plush lobby
with its buttery yellow walls and historic furniture.
Paintings of the Texas landscape brought an added
touch of the West to the decor. "So this is how the
other half lives?"

"You're part of that half now," she reminded him
with a nudge. "You have the car to prove it."

"Do you think I was trying to prove something
buying that car?" He turned to face her. "Does it
speak badly of me?"

"Linc, it's your money. You get to decide how to
spend it. Whatever makes you happy."

"This day made me happy."

Her breath caught as he reached out and pushed
a strand of hair away from her cheek. His finger
barely brushed her skin, but she felt the touch all
the way to her toes.

"That's what friends are for," she said and then
wanted to staple-shut her mouth. Linc had been
swaying closer when she spoke the words, but now
he stepped back, putting more than simply a physical distance between them.

"Thanks, Rem." He chucked her on the arm, and
she tried not to cringe. "We should get going. It's
going to be a fun drive back to Chatelaine."

"Yeah," she agreed, although ending this day with
Linc—maybe the only one she'd ever get—was the
least fun thing she could think of doing.

The return drive seemed to take no time at

all, and soon Linc pulled to a stop in front of her mother's house.

"Thanks again," he said, and the warmth in his eyes made Remi's heart ache.

"It's not going to be the same without you at GreatStore," she told him. It was the closest she felt she could get to saying she was going to miss him without revealing too much.

"It's going to be an adjustment for me, too." He scrubbed a hand over his jaw like he was trying to massage away tension.

"Are you sure it's the right decision?" she asked. It wasn't her way to challenge someone, but she'd thought Linc loved the job the way she did. "I can't imagine not having someplace to go in the morning. The routine of it relaxes me. I know that's strange, but I figured you might be able to understand."

She could feel the heat on her cheeks. Would he think she was stupid or silly for comparing the two of them? Maybe everything they had in common had been in her head.

"You're right." He gripped the steering wheel, and she let out the breath she didn't realize she was holding.

At least he didn't think she was being ridiculous.

"But I'm afraid if I stay there, I'll become complacent. I've had months to get used to my change in financial status. Until this week, I haven't done much about it."

"You've taken care of your mom," she reminded him. "That's important."

"Yes, but she doesn't need anything more from me. My brothers also plan to help her. They want a chance to contribute, and I need something new in my life. Something I choose for myself. I like working at GreatStore, but would I have picked it if I'd had other options? It's time I explore those options. The only way I'm going to do that is if my mind isn't filled with inventory, staffing issues and distribution details. I'm not moving away, Remi."

"Yet," she felt compelled to add and wondered how he would respond. To her chagrin, he didn't contradict her.

"Yet," he agreed. "It's time for me to explore what I really want to do. I've always imagined I was meant for bigger things than life had given me. No more excuses. Now is the time to make my life mean something."

His words were like a slap in the face. She'd found meaning in the little moments and had convinced herself they shared that value.

It was another reminder that she and Linc might not be made for each other the way she'd always wanted to believe. They were simply work friends. Who knew if they'd stay in touch now that he was moving on?

One fun day together clearly wasn't the start of something special the way she'd secretly hoped it might be. But in addition to lusting after him, she genuinely cared for him. She wanted Linc to be happy even if his happiness didn't involve her.

So she plastered a bright smile on her face as she placed her hand on the door latch. "Whatever you decide, I know it will be amazing. Goodbye, Linc. I had a great day."

Ugh. If this was what heartbreak felt like, she was grateful she'd never truly been in love before.

"See you around, Remi," he said.

Maybe that was a better farewell than goodbye, but it hurt just the same. She got out of the car and walked up the stone path to let herself into her childhood home.

"Remi, is that you?" her mother called from the kitchen. Even though it was just the two of them now, Stella Reynolds still loved to cook and bake. Their neighbors benefited since Stella typically made more than she and Remi could finish, even with leftovers.

Remi quickly dashed a hand across each cheek when a couple of tears spilled over.

"It's me, Mom," she called, trying to make her tone sound chipper. She walked into the kitchen. "Something smells delicious."

"We're having chicken enchiladas," Stella reported. "I made an extra batch for Mike at the post office. His wife had her baby early, so I want to give them a little break on cooking. We still have plenty. I hope you're hungry."

"Linc and I had a late lunch," Remi told her mom. "I'm not sure I'll have more than a few bites tonight, but I'd love to take the leftovers to the store for lunch tomorrow."

Stella wiped her hands on a kitchen towel as she turned. "How was your date?"

"It wasn't a date." Remi rolled her eyes. "Linc wanted a friend along when he bought his new car."

"You went to lunch after," Stella pointed out. "That means it was a lunch date."

"I don't think he thought of it that way. It's not like that between us. It never has been."

"But it could be." Stella's smile was genuine. For as long as she could remember, Remi had been told she looked like her mom. She took it as a great compliment and hoped to one day possess even half the quiet confidence of her mother. "You know your dad and I started as friends. I was his English tutor in high school. Things grew from there between us. Don't underestimate starting as friends."

Remi had heard her parents' love story many times, but she didn't say that. Stella had fallen into a bit of a depression after Remi's dad passed away.

Remi had gone to college in Oklahoma, majoring in English, and had gotten a job at a bookstore in Tulsa after graduation. But she'd returned to Chatelaine after her father's death. Her younger sisters, Leah and Livvie, were busy with their lives and didn't appreciate life in a small town the way Remi did. As the oldest, Remi felt a deep-rooted responsibility to support her mom, and working in the book department at GreatStore made her happy.

It made Stella happy to share stories about her life with her late husband and remember the good things. "You and Dad were special," she assured her mom. "I don't think Linc and I are destined for a future together."

It pained her to say the words, but she was a practical woman. It was one of the things Linc liked about her, and she had to admit she liked about herself.

The sooner she gave up on her fantasies about the two of them, the quicker she would come to terms with him no longer being a part of her life in the way she wanted. The sooner she'd find peace again.

Chapter Four

"I can't believe you actually had the *cojones* to do it. I didn't think you had it in you, Linc."

Linc glared at Damon over the hood of the Ferrari later that night. Along with Coop and Max, Damon had come over for a beer and to check out his new ride.

"What do you mean you didn't think I had it in me? I told you I had plans for the money."

Cooper snorted. "Come on, Linc. You've been feeding us that line since the summer. As much as I hate to admit it, Damon is right. This was a big step."

Linc turned to Max, who stood next to him. "Do you agree with these yahoos?"

Max shrugged. "I'm an accountant. I approve of you using discretion when spending your money."

"That's right. I was showing discretion and maturity."

"I also figured you were a big chicken," Max added.

Damon let out a whoop of laughter. Cooper squawked and did a ridiculous chicken imitation back and forth across the driveway.

"You three are the worst," Linc complained. "I should have let you play in traffic when we were kids."

"You're too responsible for that," Max told him.

"Plus, Mom would have been furious," Coop added. "It's a great car, Linc. It must be awesome to drive."

Linc crossed his arms over his chest. "It is, and if you weren't so annoying, I'd let you take it out for a spin."

"Even more fun with a pretty girl in the passenger seat." Damon winked, then held up his hands when Linc glared even harder. "Don't shoot the messenger. I have it on good authority that you were spotted with Remi Reynolds earlier today. It's not a criticism. She's awesome."

Linc wasn't sure why it bothered him to hear that people in town had taken notice of Remi and him together. They'd been friends for years. It should be no big deal. It *was* no big deal, which didn't explain his annoyance.

"She's a friend," he felt compelled to point out. "I wasn't sure if I was going to trade in the truck or would need help driving it back. It turns out, when you pay six figures for a car, the dealership makes arrangements for your old car to be delivered back to you."

"You kept the truck?" Damon asked with a smirk. "Is that the adult equivalent of a kid holding on to the side of the pool instead of diving into the deep end?"

"It's practical," Linc answered, feeling a little defensive. "I can't haul things in a Ferrari."

"For all the hauling you do." Damon doubled over in laughter.

"Let's talk more about Linc's lady friend," Coop suggested.

Damn, brothers were annoying.

"She was along for the ride." Linc shrugged. "Nothing more."

"I don't see why you wouldn't want to make it more," Cooper countered. "I've always thought there could be something between you and Remi."

"You two are like peas and carrots," Max said with his best—but still pathetic—Forrest Gump impression.

Linc felt his mouth hook up on one side as he thought about how much Remi had enjoyed his movie quote at the dealership. Would she be just as amused by his brother's?

His smile faded. The thought of her being entertained by somebody else didn't sit well, even though he knew there was nothing between them.

"I'm not in the market for a relationship, especially with somebody like Remi. She's a white-picket-fence kind of woman, and I can't give that to her. I've got to figure out what's next for me."

"You know that having a girlfriend doesn't prevent you from doing that," Coop pointed out, unhelpfully as far as Linc was concerned.

"My whole life has been about duty and thinking about what other people want and need," Linc told his brothers, frustration making his tone sharper than he meant it to be. "Is it so wrong that I want to take time for myself?"

When his brothers didn't immediately answer, Linc inwardly cursed himself. It wasn't their fault—or Justine's or his mother's—that Rick had put the weight of responsibility on Linc's thin shoulders before he walked away from their family. Linc never wanted his siblings to feel like he resented them for how his life turned out.

"It's not wrong," Damon said in an uncharacteristically serious tone.

"What are you planning to do with your money?" Linc asked his youngest brother directly, wanting the attention off himself.

"At the rate it's coming…" Damon threw up his hands. "I might be using my portion to pay for a retirement home."

Linc blew out a small laugh. Although he understood the sentiment, Damon had always had a flair for the dramatic.

It had been over six months since he'd received his inheritance. Martin Smith checked in with him on

occasion, but his grandfather's friend gave no indication of when the next installment would be distributed, which should be Max's, based on birth order.

"What if somebody contests the will?" Max
asked, voicing a concern Linc thought only he had.
"Or Martin Smith is trying to figure out a way to
keep the inheritance for himself? Justine thinks the
world of him, but what do we really know about the
guy other than he was Wendell Fortune's best friend?
How do we know we can trust him? It all seemed
clear cut in the summer, but I'm beginning to wonder with no more word from Martin."

Linc wasn't sure how to answer that question other
than with the truth. "I have a good feeling about the
guy and Justine has sharp instincts. If something
weird happens, I have enough to spread the wealth,
if you know what I mean."

Cooper shoved him harder than necessary. "It's
also no longer your job to take care of us, if you
know what I mean?"

Linc acknowledged his brother's comment with
a nod. "Old habits. Either way, you've all had plenty
of time to get used to being wealthy. You must have
thoughts on how you're going to spend your money."

He pulled the keys to the sports car from his
pocket and dangled them toward each of his brothers.
"Tell me what your first big purchase is going to
be. Whoever gives the best answer gets to drive my
sweet ride."

"Don't even bother acting like this is a competition," Damon said, shaking his head. "First, I'm guaranteed to win because neither of these two has a single ounce of creativity inside them. Second, I bet I'm the only one who can handle a Ferrari. It takes a special kind of man for this type of car."

There was a moment of silence, then Linc, Max and Cooper burst into hysterical laughter. The funniest part was that Damon was serious. He believed the line of bull he was feeding them.

"Nice try," he told his baby brother. "But you have to earn it."

"Fine," Damon agreed, then pointed at Max. "Age before beauty. How are you going to spend the money?"

Max shrugged. "I'm going to buy a house. My dream house. Maybe I'll even look in that gated community out by the LC Club. I could build something as eccentric as Wendell's castle." He raised a brow in Damon's direction. "That's creative."

"Next," Damon said to Cooper.

Cooper adjusted his Stetson and flashed his patented troublemaker grin. "I don't know. I might head to Vegas and put it all on red. I've always wanted to test my luck. This inheritance gives me the means to roll the dice."

Linc snorted. "That's the dumbest thing I've ever heard."

"Yeah," Damon agreed. "Stupid isn't the same as creative."

Cooper reached out and punched their baby

brother on the shoulder. Damon responded with a shove, but before things could escalate, Linc whistled sharply, the way he used to when they were kids and their roughhousing got out of hand.

"Let's have a beer before we hear Damon's bright idea for the money." It was in Linc's nature to defuse any sort of tension, even if he understood his brothers were grown men and probably wouldn't start rolling around in his front yard.

Max, Cooper and Damon followed him into his modest house.

A few years ago, he'd bought the twelve-hundred square foot, two bedroom rancher from one of his coworkers who'd retired and moved to Colorado to be closer to her grandkids. The decor could be described best as vintage grandma and most of his neighbors in the established community a few miles from downtown Chatelaine were decades older than Linc. He hadn't bothered to change much as saving had always been more important to Linc than spending.

Updating the house could be another project he tackled, although his thoughts went to Remi once again. Would it be too much to ask her to help him with redecorating? She always had great ideas for the displays at GreatStore, and not just in the book section.

He didn't want to overstep the bounds of their friendship, especially when he wasn't sure what to do with the new feelings he had for her.

After pulling four beers from the fridge, he

walked into the family room to find his brothers sprawled out on the lumpy old couches. New furniture was definitely in order.

"Damon, you're up," Linc said as he took a seat next to Max. "What's your big plan?"

The youngest Maloney brother ran a hand through his wavy brown hair. "Like I said, I might be old and gray before Martin shows up with my check. I've got plenty of time to come up with a plan."

The answer didn't seem to surprise any of them since, unlike Linc, Damon had never been much of a planner.

Linc wondered how to balance his need for a plan with the feeling that he should be doing something big now that he had the time and resources.

"I might go back to school," Linc said without thinking about it. He took a long pull on his beer and realized his brothers were staring at him with varying degrees of shock.

"To pick up coeds?" Damon asked after several seconds.

Linc snorted. "To finish my degree, doofus."

"Why do you need a degree?" Cooper asked. "You're rich."

Linc wasn't sure how to explain it. "I need a purpose, even with the money. I'm not interested in blowing it all on a weekend in Vegas."

"What about all the women you've never had a chance with before?" Damon gave a self-satisfied chuckle. "Maybe that's what I'm going to do. Use my money to wine and dine the girls who have been out of my league before now."

Cooper shook his head. "Bro, what woman have you wanted to date that you haven't had a chance with?"

Damon was a well-known man about town, at least in Chatelaine. His easygoing personality and natural charm made him very popular with the ladies.

"Is Christine part of why you want to go back and get your degree?" Max asked, studying the label of his beer bottle instead of looking directly at Linc.

Linc hated that his brother had guessed his motivation, but he didn't deny it. His high school girlfriend and first and only love had broken up with him shortly after he dropped out of college and returned to work full-time at GreatStore. She'd told him she had no time for a guy with no future or real prospects.

He'd buried his hurt when it threatened to turn into resentment toward his family. It wasn't anyone's fault that he couldn't handle the cost of school and help his mom financially. It certainly hadn't been his plan, but that was reality.

He hadn't realized he was still hung up on the rejection until now.

Although maybe "hung up" wasn't the right way to describe how he felt. He'd gotten over Christine. He'd even seen her a couple of times over the years when she'd returned to town to visit her family. His heart no longer ached, but his pride hadn't overcome the hit.

"I want to own my own business," he explained to

his brothers. "I want something that belongs to me, but I'm not sure I'm cut out for being an entrepreneur or running a company. Having a degree might help me clarify what comes next."

"Let me get this straight. You want to use your money to work harder?" Damon looked stunned. "What kind of glutton for punishment are you?"

"That's not how I see it," Linc said with a sigh.

"But those are facts," Damon insisted.

"I think Linc is on to something," Max offered.

Linc nodded at his closest-in-age brother. "Thanks, man."

"You've always been a boring stick in the mud." Max winked. "It makes sense that the way you choose to spend your money would reflect that."

Linc scratched his nose with his middle finger. "Always got my back, Max. Appreciate it."

"I'm joking," Max told him. "You can do whatever you want with the money. We all get that choice. You've paid off Mom's house, which is a huge gift to her."

"I want to get her a new car," Cooper announced.

"I'm going to send her on a beach vacation," Damon offered. "When was the last time Mom's been on a trip?"

They were all silent for several moments. Linc couldn't remember their mom ever taking a true vacation. Sometimes she needed a break from work, but there hadn't been the time or money for big vacations to Disney World or the national parks.

All they'd managed as a family were a few weekend excursions to the beach near Corpus Christi and weekend fishing at Lake Chatelaine. Linc appreciated that he and his siblings would have the means to make their mother's life easier. Kimberly wasn't perfect, and she was still working on repairing her relationship with Justine.

Her harsh reaction to his sister's decision to become a mom before Justine and Stefan had rediscovered each other had made things strained, but he felt confident they would get over it. It was hard to imagine either of them holding on to the past when Morgan was so important to them both.

The money would not only benefit each of them individually. It would give them a chance to come together in a new way as a family. He liked to think that Wendell Fortune would have approved. Perhaps the grandfather he'd never known would have wanted his wealth to play that role in his grandchildren's lives.

"What do you think Dad would have thought about the money?" Damon asked, seemingly out of nowhere, although the question made sense to Linc since he'd been mulling over family bonds. "Do you think Rick would have stayed if things hadn't been a struggle with so many kids and so little money?"

They fell silent, contemplating private thoughts about their father and his choices. Those decisions had a massive effect on the men they'd become.

Linc guessed his brothers felt the same way as

he did, which was resistant to giving the father who deserted them any credit in their lives.

Eventually, his brothers looked to him for an answer. He understood. As the oldest, he had the most precise recollections of their dad. Damon had been only two when Rick left, and Justine still a sparkle in her mother's eye.

Even though Linc remembered his father, the crystal clear moments in his mind didn't provide many answers. Mostly he remembered his father's restlessness.

Rick's impatience hadn't exactly taken the form of a short fuse or a snappish tone. No, it was more like Linc had always sensed that his father had someplace else he wanted to be.

He wondered now if he'd made that up in his head, part of his origin story, but he didn't think so. Kids noticed things. They picked up on the moods of the adults around them, sometimes more clearly than the adults themselves.

Linc didn't have much experience with babies or little children, but he'd seen the dynamic play out plenty of times in the GreatStore aisles. He and his brothers didn't discuss their father or his leaving in detail. It was a fact of their lives.

Although it was undeniable, he didn't want to give Rick any credit or acknowledge his influence. "I don't think it would have changed anything," he told his brothers. "Maybe coming into an inheritance would have prompted him to leave earlier. Dad felt trapped, and that didn't come from too many kids. It came from inside of him."

Each of his brothers seemed to find relief in his assessment of the situation. Damon let out an audible sigh, and Coop's shoulders relaxed.

Max placed his beer bottle on the coffee table. "I'm not going to say I'm glad the man is dead, because he doesn't mean that much to me, but I'm grateful the money is coming to us and not him. It'll take time for us to decide exactly how we want to live now that we're filthy rich, but we'll figure it out. And we'll take care of each other along the way. All Rick Maloney cared about was himself."

The rest of them nodded at Max's words.

"I wish I could say something good about our father," Linc admitted. "After all, Wendell Fortune didn't treat him much better than he treated us."

Cooper shook his head. "Being a deadbeat dad to one kid after a surprise pregnancy makes Wendell Fortune a jerk. Five kids don't happen by accident. Dad should've thought of the consequences of his actions before he took them."

Linc raised his beer bottle in salute to that comment, then drained the golden liquid. For some reason, he thought of Remi again. She was always so kind to the kids of their coworkers who came into the store and loved helping young shoppers pick out the perfect book or toy when she covered that department. He had no doubt she'd make a good mom one day and was surprised she hadn't already found a guy to settle down with and start a family.

Thinking of Remi with another man caused a sensation to bubble up inside him that was both shocking and unfamiliar. He immediately squashed the emotion, which felt like a combination of jealousy and yearning he'd never associated with himself.

He chalked them up to the uncertainty he felt about his future and indecision concerning what to do with the money. That had to be it. He didn't want to be a family man.

Grabbing the remote from the arm of the sofa, he flipped on the TV. "How about I use some of my inheritance to order pizza? We can watch a game."

His suggestion was met with a round of cheers. "I'll grab more beer," Damon said as he popped up from the couch. "No black olives on the pizza."

Max was already tapping away on his phone. "Extra black olives," he called. "Got it."

Linc smiled at the banter that flew back and forth between the brothers. He would give more attention to his future when he was alone with his thoughts.

He was at a crossroads in deciding what should come next in his life, but he knew he couldn't let himself forget what mattered. His family and the people he cared about. Everything else could be managed along the journey.

He silently thanked the grandfather he'd never get a chance to meet in person for making the journey way more fun.

Chapter Five

Three days later, Remi looked up from the bowl of oatmeal on the table as her mom walked into the kitchen.

"Morning," she mumbled, listlessly stirring her breakfast.

"What has my sunny girl looking so glum today?" Stella dropped a kiss on Remi's head before moving toward the coffee maker.

"I'm not glum," Remi lied. "It's just another boring workday. Same old thing."

"I've never heard you describe working with books as boring," her mother pointed out. "Does this have anything to do with the fact that Lincoln Maloney is no longer at GreatStore?"

"Lincoln *Fortune* Maloney," Remi clarified. "I'm

happy for Linc and the newfound freedom to change
his whole life, but it isn't the same without him."

"You realize you can see him even if you don't
work together anymore?" Stella took her time pouring coffee, then added a scant drop of half-and-half
to the cup. "Chatelaine is a small town. The two of
you are friends regardless of your status as coworkers. Based on your date this week, I thought that
might be turning into more."

Remi pointed the spoon at her mother. "Why am
I the one who gets accused of living in a fantasy
world? Is it because of my love of reading? Linc
doesn't think of me that way, Mom. I thought I was
okay with it. I am okay. It's an adjustment not having him around."

"In what way?"

"The store isn't the same without him." Nothing
was the same, and Remi was struggling to overcome
her sadness.

Her mom was a hopeless romantic who believed
in true love after many years of being happily married to Remi's dad. Remi felt foolish admitting how
much she'd come to rely on Linc being a part of her
almost daily life.

"It's a small town," her mother repeated.

"I saw him yesterday," Remi said, almost to herself.

Her mom beamed. "Well, there you go."

Remi picked up her uneaten oatmeal and pushed
back from the table. "Let me clarify. I saw his car,

which is hard to miss on the streets of Chatelaine. He didn't see me."

She flashed a self-deprecating smile, even though she was already dumping out her oatmeal at the sink. "He's hard to miss now, and I'm still easy to overlook."

She heard the scuff of a chair on the tile floor. A moment later, Stella's soft arms came around her shoulders. "You are not easy to overlook. You are amazing, my sweet girl, and I know there's someone special out there for you. Maybe the timing hasn't been right or it's not Linc, but that doesn't mean you won't find your perfect match in the future. When it comes to love, my instincts are perfect."

Remi smiled and swallowed down the ball of regret that bloomed in her chest. The timing hadn't been right because she was a wimp who'd never put herself out there. "You're the best, Mom. No matter what happens next, I know how lucky I am to have you in my corner."

After the conversation with Stella, Remi managed to pull herself out of her funk by the time she got to work.

She spent the morning taking care of inventory. The amount of space in the section was being decreased again, so she did her best to make the one aisle she had look attractive and cheery.

The interim manager from a store in San Antonio who was filling in until they found a permanent replacement for Linc didn't appreciate the importance of books or understand why she fought so hard for square footage. She wanted to display them in a way that would be appealing to customers and draw more people toward the area.

But she refused to let her shrinking department size get her down. Remi had always made the best of whatever circumstances life gave her. The talk with her mom reminded her that her current challenges were no exception.

She might not have Stella's faith that she was destined to find her perfect match, but Remi had a good life even without love in it.

She and Linc had often taken their breaks together in a quiet corner of the stockroom, but it felt lonely to be there on her own with him gone. So when her lunch half-hour arrived, she sat at one of the tables in the employee lounge, listening to the conversation flow around her.

There were enough people on the GreatStore staff, like Alana, who loved chatting that Remi didn't have to add much. She enjoyed the debates and chitchat without inserting herself, listening with half an ear and letting her thoughts wander.

"So are you and Richie Rich Fortune Malone an official item?" Paul asked as he plopped down next to her. "I heard you were the inspiration for that sweet ride he brought home."

Remi choked on the bite of apple she'd just taken. "I wasn't his inspiration for anything. Linc bought the car on his own. I was there to—"

"Make sure he didn't buy two," Alana called from the next table over.

"That's too bad," Paul answered. "If he'd bought two cars, maybe he'd loan one to me."

"I'd volunteer as your copilot," Alana told him.

Remi kept a smile on her face even though that was the opposite of how she felt. She didn't want to be joking about Linc or his car or her role in his life. Because she knew Paul had to be joking when he suggested they could be an item.

"You guys don't work together anymore," Paul said, as if he could read her mind. He'd lowered his voice so only she could hear. "What's stopping you from taking things to the next level?"

Remi was having trouble controlling her breathing. "The most pertinent reason is that Linc doesn't see me in that way."

"He doesn't *not* see you like that. If you let him know it's what you want, maybe something more could happen."

Remi had thought Paul was speaking quietly enough that only she could hear, but a couple of people sitting at their table nodded. Alana got up from her chair and took the seat across from Remi.

"Right now is your chance," her friend urged. "Make your move, girl. Linc is a hottie. His brothers, too. That family won the genetic lottery."

Paul made a gagging sound.

"It's true," Alana told him. "The Fortune Maloneys could give the Hemsworth brothers a run for their money."

Remi heard somebody murmur "Amen," but she was too busy trying to control the blush she could feel staining her cheeks to determine who'd said it.

"Besides, he's rich now." Alana wiggled her delicate brows. "Who doesn't want to date a wealthy guy? Sign me up, please."

Remi shook her head. "Wanting to date Linc has nothing to do with his money. I like him for who he is."

"So you admit you have it bad for him?" Alana looked pleased as punch that Remi had finally confirmed her suspicions.

Remi glanced around the room. All eyes were on her. "Is there anyone who doesn't realize I have a crush on Linc?" Mortification threatened to overtake her.

Paul gave her shoulder a reassuring pat. "If it makes you feel any better—and I'm not sure why it would— I don't think Linc has a clue."

Remi hadn't recognized the hope that sprouted inside her chest until Paul's words dashed it. For a split second, she'd thought there could be more to him taking her to lunch, the way her mother suspected. "Exactly. He doesn't have any idea because he doesn't feel the same."

She rose from her chair and made a point of glancing at the clock that hung on the break room wall. "I've got to get back on the floor. Please, no one tell Linc about this. I don't want him to know. I like being his friend, and it would change everything if he knew my feelings were more. He's moving on with his life. I'm happy for him. I want him to be happy. I don't want it to be awkward if he comes by the store again."

She paused to take a breath and noticed the whole room was staring at her.

Alana rose and moved to stand next to Remi. "Your secret is safe with us," she said, and no one contradicted her. "Even if we're secretly hoping you change your mind and climb that cutie Fortune like a spider monkey."

Remi laughed, although the tips of her ears grew hot. She was blushing from head to toe. "I have work to do," she said and hurried from the room.

The faster she walked across the store, the more it felt as though tears stung the back of her eyes. She hadn't minded her crush on Linc when it was a secret. It was like losing herself in a story. Her harmless fantasies kept her entertained, and no one else had to know.

But they did know. Now she was going to have to find a way to move on. Remi might not have Alana's effervescent personality, but she liked to believe she possessed a sort of quiet pride.

She wasn't going to allow everyone she knew to feel sorry for her as she watched Linc move on with his exciting new adventures while she not-so-secretly pined for him. Even she wasn't that much of a glutton for punishment.

She'd just reached the book aisle when her phone pinged with an incoming text. It was a group chat, the same one Linc had used to invite them all to his New Year's Eve party.

He'd rented the Silver Dollar Theater, Chatelaine's single-screen movie house, for Friday night and invited all his friends from GreatStore to join him.

Remi would have preferred if the invitation had come to her exclusively but reminded herself that she was giving up her girlish crush on Lincoln Fortune Maloney. Friday night would be the perfect opportunity to prove to her friends and herself that she was over him.

Or at least heading in that direction.

Her heart ached at the thought, but she pressed a hand to her chest and told herself it was for the best. She began straightening the new releases, letting her fingers move over the embossed print on the shiny front covers.

Stick to fantasies between the covers of a book, she silently told herself. It was the only way to ensure she didn't get hurt.

As he sat in the lobby of the Silver Dollar Theater Friday night, Linc was shocked at how much he looked forward to his movie party. He'd resisted the urge to stop by GreatStore that week…barely. He could have found plenty of excuses since it was the only big-box store in town, but he felt too foolish.

He wouldn't have been going for any real purpose other than to visit his friends and former coworkers.

What kind of a man made a big to-do about quitting his job to move on only to keep returning to the company? He'd be hovering around like a helicopter parent who couldn't admit he wasn't needed anymore.

It had nothing to do with the belief that the temporary manager or his former coworkers couldn't handle things without him. His ego wasn't that grand.

He missed the camaraderie. If he was being completely honest, he specifically missed Remi. That fact alone had kept him away more than anything else. He'd never given his feelings for his sweet friend much thought. She'd simply been a part of his life.

His brother Damon had helped him create a profile on one of the more popular dating apps. But Linc couldn't bring himself to swipe left or right on any of the women whom the algorithm deemed a match. He'd never struggled with dating before. It had been effortless and casual. For some unknown reason, dating now felt like neither of those adjectives.

He couldn't admit this entire evening had been scheduled so he could see Remi. Not to ask her out on a date. If he wanted to do that, he would have by now.

No. Linc needed to clear his head of her. He figured she would come in with the group, and they'd hang out like old times. Then the strange thrumming in his heart that had started with their dance on New Year's Eve would dissolve. They could go back to normal. He could move on with things.

He stood to greet his friends as they began to arrive. Paul and Alec were the first through the door.

The three of them had met for a beer a couple of nights ago at the Chatelaine Bar and Grill where Damon worked as a bartender. It took its inspiration from the town's mining history with a heavy timber door, tin ceilings and framed photographs marking various moments in the past. The rugged wooden bar was situated at the back of the restaurant, the piece salvaged from a saloon and adding to the ambiance.

His brother wasn't on that night, so Linc bought the first round, but when he'd tried to tell the bartender to start a tab with his credit card, Paul and Alec had shaken their heads.

"We'll take turns," Paul had said, Alec nodding like they'd worked out the plan earlier.

Even though a couple of beers and a big plate of nachos wouldn't have made a dent in his bank account, he'd appreciated that they wanted to hang out because they were friends and not because he could now treat. Though they'd made plenty of jokes about his car, he trusted that money wouldn't change their friendship.

"What have you been up to as a man of leisure?" Alec asked now as he grabbed a box of popcorn from the counter. Linc had preordered snacks and drinks for tonight. He didn't want any questions about who was paying.

"I enrolled in a business class at the UT Corpus Christi campus."

Paul and Alec looked shocked. "I thought you were joking about going back to school," Paul told him.

"Why do you need to go to school?" Alec demanded. "You're rich."

"I can't sit around counting my money and watching the Syfy channel every day."

The two friends continued to stare. "Why not?" Paul asked after a few seconds. "That sounds perfect."

Linc laughed. "Trust me. It gets old real quick." This week had shown him that. He still had no idea what he wanted to do or what type of business he might like to own but figured a class was a step in the right direction. Any direction.

More people entered the theater, and he couldn't help but notice Remi wasn't among the group. She'd responded on the group chat that she was coming tonight. Had she changed her mind?

It was good to see his friends and hear about the latest news from the store. There seemed to be some concern about corporate types hovering around earlier that week. He wished he could give his former employees some clue about the purpose of a visit from the corporate office, but he had no idea.

"Probably just first quarter planning," he suggested, hoping that was the case. Employees got nervous when corporate started sniffing around a location. But he knew GreatStore in Chatelaine performed well.

The theater manager announced the start of the movie, and everyone began filing into the theater.

Linc continued to hang back, glancing at the door.

"She'll be here," Alec said as he grabbed another popcorn box.

"I don't know what you're talking about." Linc shrugged. "I'm the host, so I just want to make sure everyone gets a good seat."

"Right." Alec lobbed a piece of popcorn in Linc's direction. "Stop watching for Remi. She said she was coming and she will. She's dependable that way."

Linc nodded but didn't immediately answer his friend. He wasn't sure when dependable had become exciting, but his heart thumped wildly at the thought of seeing her tonight.

"It's fine. Maybe she had something come up."

"What comes up on a typical Friday night in Chatelaine?" Alec asked with a snort. "Going to the movies is the most exciting thing this town has to offer."

Paul snickered. "I don't know. That group of guys staying at the LC Club for a bachelor party came into the store earlier today. One of them was flirting with Remi pretty hard. Who buys a book on their way to a bachelor party unless they're trying to impress the woman selling it?"

Alana, who was at the back of the group, looked

over her shoulder. "That dude was so obvious, although I'm not sure Remi had any clue as to his intentions. She legit believed he wanted reading material during a weekend with his buddies."

Linc forced a smile, although he couldn't stop thinking about Remi choosing an evening with some stranger instead of coming to his movie party. Hell, he felt pathetic but reminded himself they were friends. She could do anything she wanted or go out with any guy who interested her.

He'd seen several customers flirt with her in the store over the years, although she hadn't given any of them the time of day as far as he could tell.

Things changed. He was no longer part of her life in a meaningful way, and it wasn't his business.

He grabbed a box of popcorn, followed his friends, and took a seat at the end of the aisle.

Just before the lights dimmed, Remi hurried into the theater.

"Sorry I'm late," she called as everyone turned to watch her entrance. "One of the pipes in my mom's kitchen burst."

Linc's wildly beating heart settled in his chest. She headed for an open seat a couple of rows in front of him, but there was a surge of activity amongst the rest of the moviegoers as people jumped up and moved around.

The next thing he knew, Alana pointed to the suddenly empty seat next to Linc. "Right here, Remi. We've got your seat saved."

Pink bloomed on Remi's cheeks, and Linc noticed she didn't quite make eye contact as she scooted past and into the seat next to him.

He couldn't hide the grin that split his face and quickly made an announcement welcoming his friends to movie night. "I remember how tired we all got at the end of a long work week. Back when I was at GreatStore—"

"A long, long time ago," somebody shouted to resounding laughter.

"Not that long ago," Linc corrected. "But I always wanted to give you all a fun start to the weekend. I'm glad I have the means to do that now and hope you enjoy the movie."

His former coworkers cheered, and he took his seat as the theater went dark.

He noticed Remi wiping her hand on the edge of her jeans. "Did you fix the pipe yourself?" he asked.

"It wasn't difficult. My dad taught me the basics of home maintenance before I left for college. He thought it was important that I be able to take care of things on my own."

"You could have called or texted me," he told her. "I would have been happy to help."

She stared up at him from beneath her lashes. Had she always had such long lashes?

"It's okay, Linc. I'm not your responsibility."

He knew that. The funny thing was, he couldn't quite explain or stop the urge to want her to be.

He tipped the popcorn box in her direction, and if

she noticed the conflicting emotions rushing through him, she didn't say a word.

"Movie popcorn is the best." She paused with her hand halfway to her mouth.

"What's wrong?"

She gave a small shake of her head. "I forgot to ask. Is this a scary movie?"

"Yeah," he answered slowly. "I mentioned movie night to Paul and Alec earlier this week. A horror flick was Paul's request."

"Oh."

"You don't like scary movies? How did I not know that? I should have picked something with witches and wizards."

"It's fine," she said. "I can always close my eyes."

"If it bothers you, we could—"

Alec turned from his seat in the row in front of them. "Quiet. I'm going to miss the cheesy dialogue with you two yapping."

"It's fine," Remi repeated in a hushed voice. She placed a hand on Linc's arm and smiled. "I'm sure I'll be—"

The next moment she jumped and let out a tiny scream when the masked stalker jumped out from behind a tree. The box of popcorn flew into the air and exploded everywhere as Linc made a grab for it.

Chapter Six

Remi wished for the sticky floor of the movie theater to open and swallow her whole. Linc must think her the world's biggest nincompoop, as her grandmother was fond of saying. She tried to sweep the scattered popcorn off his lap. When her fingers trailed over the thick denim of his fly, she snatched her hand away like she'd been scalded.

First, she'd made a fool of herself with her overactive startle reflex, then spilled popcorn all over him, and now she was copping a feel. She should have taken the broken pipe as a sign and skipped movie night. She could imagine Linc wishing she'd done exactly that.

Instead, she'd replaced the pipe in record time. Her father would have been proud, although he also would have laughed at her motivation.

"I was getting full anyway," Linc said close to her ear, and she could hear the smile in his voice.

"I'm so sorry." She ordered her nerves to calm, unsure whether she was reacting more to the movie or being so close to Linc in the dark theater. Surrounded by coworkers, she inwardly reminded herself.

She sat back in her seat, prepared to endure the rest of the horror film like a non-sissy adult, only to realize that Linc's arm had come to rest on the back of her seat. His fingertips traced circles on her shoulder as she relaxed against him.

"Remember, it's all fake," he told her. She didn't want to believe anything about this moment was less than completely real. How often in the past few years had she gone to the movies with a friend or her mother and seen couples cuddling? She'd imagined Linc next to her just as he was right now.

Chances were good that he was only comforting a nervous friend. As usual, Remi's imagination had a mind of its own. She even managed to shift a little closer without being too obvious.

The movie had an over-the-top plot about a boy who'd gone missing from summer camp decades earlier and was now terrorizing modern-day camp counselors in various clichéd—but shocking for Remi—ways. In the warm cocoon of Linc's embrace, she made it through two more startling death scenes with only a subtle flinch.

"I'm proud of you," he said against her hair. Was it her imagination, or had he also moved closer?

She could feel the heat of him and smell the scent of his clean soap mixed with buttery popcorn.

She wore a bulky sweater, but her skin seemed to tingle where their arms touched.

"It's not so bad, is it?" he said as the movie progressed.

"It's amazing," she responded, earning a low chuckle from Linc. Did he realize she was talking about the two of them and not the movie?

She barely registered the action on screen, acutely aware of the connection that seemed to be intensifying between her and Linc.

Turning her head to meet his gaze, Remi saw that his green eyes were filled with a heat she'd only dreamed of.

He said her name like it was a revelation. As if he was finally noticing her in the way she'd always wanted him to.

Her gaze strayed to his mouth and his full, perfect lips that had been wasted on a man. But they weren't wasted if he was about to kiss her. He leaned in so close their breath mingled. He was definitely going to kiss her.

Remi made the mistake of glancing at the screen at the exact moment the knife-wielding villain jumped at the movie's protagonist, and she practically leaped out of her seat and screamed.

Alana grabbed her hand, and Linc pulled away.

"You are freaking me out, girl," Alana admonished. "I'm going to pinch you every time something scary happens. Otherwise, I'm going to pee my pants by the time this movie is over."

Remi struggled to catch her breath, which she knew was more a result of what had almost occurred between her and Linc than the movie. *Almost* because she'd messed up the whole moment.

As she looked in his direction, Linc rose from the seat. "I'm going to grab a soda. You need anything?"

"No."

He turned and headed up the aisle. Remi wanted to follow—to apologize, explain, and most importantly, to find out if she'd imagined that almost kiss. But Alana still held her hand, gripping tightly as the music signaled another terrifying scene on the way.

Even if Linc had been lost in the moment, Remi had ruined it. As the body count mounted on-screen, the seat beside her remained empty, and it felt as though her heart was just as abandoned.

Linc returned as the credits rolled. The lights went up in the theater, and her coworkers surged forward to thank Linc for the evening of entertainment.

Plans were made to head over to the local bar, but Remi excused herself and headed for her car. She'd been content to be Linc's friend for so many years. Why did it have to change now?

Tears threatened as she shoved her key in the ignition. She watched the group exit the theater and head down the sidewalk. Allison, one of the newer cashiers taking a semester off from college to make money, walked next to Linc. Their arms brushed, and the extroverted newcomer smiled up at him, then laughed at something he said.

For all Remi knew, he was telling Allison about what he'd endured trying to keep Remi from losing it during the movie. Her heart sank as she watched him put an arm around Allison's shoulder, much like he had with Remi earlier.

It convinced her that the moment they'd shared had been in her mind.

She banged the heel of her palm against her head and commanded herself to start living in reality. Linc hadn't been interested in her when he was a regular guy. He certainly wouldn't be now, considering he was wealthy beyond what she could imagine and had the Fortune name to open new doors.

Swallowing back tears, she put the car into gear and headed for home and her books. At least a good story never let her down.

Linc got out of his truck in the GreatStore parking lot later that week, wondering when he'd become such a glutton for punishment.

"Where's the Ferrari?" Alec asked as he walked toward him. "I thought you would have sent this heap to the junkyard."

Linc held his hands over the driver's-side mirror. "Don't listen to him. You are gorgeous." He grinned at his friend. "I'm here for some shelves, so I needed more cargo room than a sports car gives me."

Alec rolled his eyes. "You don't like being recognized in town because it makes you feel like a celebrity. You can't fool me."

Linc sighed. "I feel like a celebrity and not in a good way. Would you believe I've gotten calls from ten people in my graduating class since they found out about the inheritance? I've never had so many offers to go out to lunch or skeet shooting. One guy suggested we head to Cabo for the weekend because he saw on TV that they're doing a wet T-shirt contest at one of the bars. He thought I would fly him to Mexico to ogle women in see-through shirts."

"Clearly not somebody who was a close friend of yours in high school," Alec said with a laugh. "Otherwise, he would have known that wouldn't be something you'd go for."

"Who'd go for that?" Frustration at his current circumstance pounded through Linc. The inheritance was supposed to give him freedom. Instead, he barely left his house for fear of being waylaid by people who wanted something from him. "Why would I spend my money that way?"

"Word's gotten out on exactly how much money you inherited."

"Nobody knows how much money I inherited other than my family."

"True," Alec agreed as they started toward the front entrance. "You might want to share the details with your closest friends. Paul and I have a wager on how many zeros were included."

"I'm not telling you."

"I figured as much. It's fine so long as you don't tell him, either."

"Trust me. It's better that you don't know. People can't try to get the information out of you."

"A few already have." Alec shrugged and looked at the ground. "Mostly, they're going after Remi. You'd think half the town of Chatelaine made a New Year's resolution to start a book club based on the number of people meandering through her section. A lot of them want to pump her for info on you."

"What are you talking about?" Linc demanded, anger on Remi's behalf pounding through him along with a strange surge of protectiveness. "Why would anybody bother Remi to ferret out details about me?"

"Because you like her."

"I like a lot of people."

Paul waved from the side of the loading dock, where he supervised a flatbed of merchandise coming into the store.

Alec waved him over. "Settle a debate for us, man. Can you guess why people are trying to get to Linc through Remi now that he's a hot commodity?"

"He was a hot commodity before," Paul said, pointing at Linc. "No offense, but I never understood your appeal with the ladies. You're good-looking, but you're boring as hell."

Linc felt his mouth drop open. "I'm not boring. I never was boring."

"Remi likes boring." Alec gestured toward Paul, who nodded in agreement.

"Remi and I are friends," Linc insisted. "There's no reason for anyone to invent something more between us. It's not true."

"Only because you won't man up and ask her out," Paul told him.

"Why am I friends with the two of you? There are plenty of people in town I can hang out with and not get this kind of grief."

"They only want you for your dollar bills. I saw Cooper the other day." Paul winked. "He agrees with us."

"I'm going to drive over to Corpus Christi to get the shelves I need or have them delivered. That way, I won't have to listen to this nonsense anymore. My brothers know I'm not planning to settle down."

"Who's talking about settling down?" Paul countered.

"You're getting ahead of yourself," Alec agreed, rolling his dark eyes toward the pale blue winter sky. "You could take her to dinner—and not with a sorry excuse about needing help picking out a car. Who needs help spending money on a Ferrari?"

"It wasn't a bogus reason, and she was a huge help."

"Because you like her." Paul gave Alex an annoying high five. "He might be rich, but we're smarter." He turned back to Linc. "It's dinner. Ask her to dinner." Paul spoke at a measured pace, as if Linc would be slow to catch on.

That wasn't exactly untrue.

"Have a good time," Alec told him. "Live a little. When was the last time you wined and dined a woman?"

"That's not my style."

"So get a new style. Also, it would help if you worked on a wardrobe upgrade," Alex said. "Those sneakers have seen better days."

"I'm leaving. Forget it." Linc had a feeling his current aggravation might have something to do with his friends being right, but he wasn't about to admit it. "What time do you guys get off?"

"Six," Paul told him.

Alec nodded. "Me, too. Want to watch a game tonight?"

Linc shook his head. "No. I'm coming back to the store to buy shelves when you two aren't here, so you won't bother me." He opened the door of his truck to climb in.

"Ask her out," Paul called. "Don't be a chicken."

Without turning, Linc raised one hand and flipped them a different kind of bird.

He got in his truck and headed for…well, he wasn't sure where to go. The shelves were supposed to keep him busy for the afternoon. But he wasn't going to take that kind of grief from anyone. What did his friends know anyway?

He and Remi were fine as friends. It was comfortable. Easy, uncomplicated. No significant effort or responsibilities needed.

He hated that it made him sound like his father,

the last person he wanted to take after in life. Even more, he hated the thought that people might be bothering Remi to get to him.

He would have to talk to her about it. Maybe over dinner. Friends had dinner together, and despite what Paul and Alex believed, friendship was all he had to offer Remi.

Chapter Seven

"How's your dinner? You haven't eaten much."

Remi's fingers tightened around her fork as she smiled at the man sitting across from her at the LC Club on Saturday night. "The chicken is so tender. I'm savoring each bite." As if to prove her point, she forked up a giant piece. Shoving it into her mouth, she closed her eyes and feigned delight as she chewed, even though the meat tasted like rubber.

Andrew Rhodes, her date for the evening, nodded his approval when she met his gaze again. She'd met him at GreatStore last weekend when he'd come in to pick up supplies for a bachelor party weekend at the LC Club. She'd been covering multiple sections because a few coworkers were out sick, and Andrew and his buddies had flirted shamelessly. That had been Friday afternoon before the movie party, and she'd barely given him a second glance.

All of her focus had been on Linc, which left her with nothing but disappointment and a crick in her neck from staying up late reading.

When Andrew returned to the store during her Sunday shift, he'd bought a half dozen books at her recommendation. He'd also asked her to dinner since he was driving back down to the LC Club from San Antonio the following weekend.

Remi had been asked out more than once over the years, but she'd always said no. And she'd been about to politely decline Andrew's invitation when the image of Linc and his arm around the cute cashier after the movie had popped into her brain.

So here she was on a date with a reasonably attractive man at the nicest restaurant in the county, and all she could think of was Linc. Andrew had dark hair and a lean build with honey-colored eyes. He did something with investments in San Antonio, although Remi was having trouble pretending she was interested in his never-ending stream of office stories.

"This is a halfway decent place for a town like Chatelaine," Andrew said, glancing around the restaurant with its dark wood and ambient lighting. "I almost made a reservation at the Saddle and Spur, but I left my cowboy boots at home this trip."

Remi felt like she should be offended on behalf of her community but couldn't muster the energy for it. She knew she had to put aside her silly crush on Lincoln once and for all, but it was clear that accepting a date with a random man would not be the way to find peace.

At least not this man.

"Tonight is my first time dining at the club," she told Andrew, forcing a smile. "I was here for a New Year's Eve party. They have great food."

"It's not exactly Michelin star worthy." Andrew said. "But it's fine, and the company is even better."

"Better than fine." Remi lifted a brow. "That's high praise."

Andrew had the courtesy to look slightly abashed. "I like you, Remi. By the way you handled a bunch of goofy guys in the store last weekend, I could tell that there was more to you than your shy and innocent act. Still waters run deep and all that, you know?"

Did she know? Was her shyness an act? She'd never thought of it that way. But she'd accepted herself for who she was and didn't feel like she needed to pretend to be bubbly or more outgoing to please anyone else.

As much as she didn't think there'd be a love connection between her and Andrew, she appreciated that he'd asked her out and was clearly interested in her. That was more than she could say for some people.

Despite her feelings for Linc and her doubts about Andrew, she owed it to him and herself to give this date a real shot.

"What did you think about the books I recommended? Which one are you going to start first? They're all amazing in different ways."

He took a small sip of the bourbon he'd ordered. Remi hadn't been sure what to think of a man who made a big deal about a restaurant not stocking his favorite brand of liquor, but Andrew had found something he liked on the LC Club's list. Of course, most of the guys she knew in Chatelaine were strictly beer drinkers.

Andrew had laughed when she'd marveled over the giant square of ice accompanying his drink. Apparently, that was a trend in high-end establishments. She might not be the most experienced person, but she was learning.

"Can I be honest?" He ran a finger over the rim of the bourbon glass.

"I hope so."

"I'm not much of a reader, Remi. The truth is I faked interest in those books to have an excuse to talk to you."

"Oh. I suppose that's flattering. Although, now that you have the books, you might try reading." She flashed a smile. "It's a very good selection."

"I haven't read a book since college," he said. "Even then, I used Cliffs Notes as often as possible."

She had trouble keeping her smile in place. It was disappointing, though she supposed many people felt that way. It wasn't as if the book section at Great-Store did a bustling business.

Most of the customers who'd come by in the past couple of weeks seemed more interested in grilling her over what she knew about Linc and his inheritance than selecting a book to enjoy.

"Remi, how nice to see you."

Remi did a double take as she glanced up into Kimberly Maloney's kind face and noticed Linc standing behind his mother, looking less than pleased to see her.

Kimberly's gaze tracked between her and Andrew. "Isn't this restaurant lovely?" Kimberly held her purse tight against her. "It's almost too fancy for the likes of me. Lincoln insisted on taking me out to dinner."

"I recommend the chicken," Remi told the older woman. "You look pretty tonight, Mrs. Maloney. Is that a new dress?"

Kimberly flashed a smile as she brushed a hand over the simple, high-waisted frock. "It is and thank you. I'll take note of the chicken dish." Kimberly's gaze slid once more to Andrew.

His smile looked forced, which was not a point in his favor. Kimberly was a nice woman. Remi knew from Linc that his mom sometimes struggled with a bit of social anxiety. But she'd always gone out of her way to be kind to Remi. In fact, she came to the store to buy a few books every month and then donated them to the local library when she finished.

She'd told Remi it was her way of giving back because reading had been an important part of her life.

"I'm glad we saw you here." Kimberly leaned closer, and Remi couldn't help noticing that Linc was positively scowling now. "I wanted to thank you again for saving that copy of the new book in the Knit or Die cozy mystery series for me. I don't usually let myself splurge on hardcovers, but the discount made it a treat."

"Of course," Remi answered. "Hardcovers are special." Some of the books had gone on sale after the new year, and she'd put aside a copy of the latest from one of Kimberly's favorite authors. Technically, that was against store policy, but Remi had done it anyway.

"Your recommendation of that new thriller was perfect for Lincoln as well." She mentioned the title. "We were talking about it on the way over. He's almost finished, aren't you, sweetie?"

Linc ran a hand through his hair and looked vaguely embarrassed. "Yeah. I have some time on my hands at the moment."

Andrew chuckled. "Oh, man. That's one of the books I got from Remi last weekend, and I haven't managed to take it out of the bag." He winked at Remi. "I guess I'd rather take the pretty bookseller to dinner than spend my nights alone reading."

Now Linc's jaw went tight and a muscle ticked in his cheek. "Come on, Mom. We should get to our table."

Kimberly looked like she wanted to argue with Andrew but only pursed her lips.

"Reading is one of my favorite pastimes," Remi said, offering Linc what she hoped was an apologetic smile. "I stayed up till two in the morning reading that one over the Christmas holiday."

Andrew picked up his bourbon glass and saluted her. "Maybe we can find a better way to keep you busy in the wee hours."

Remi lowered her gaze to the table. Had her date just made a sex joke in front of Kimberly Maloney? How mortifying.

"Sleep is important," Linc's mother said in her gentle voice, and Remi wasn't sure whether she purposely misunderstood the comment or chose to ignore it. Another glance at Linc's stony features told her that he hadn't misunderstood Andrew's subtle innuendo.

"You two enjoy your dinner," he said and ushered his mom away before the conversation could get any more awkward, as if that were possible.

Andrew grinned. "There really isn't much going on in this town if all you people have to talk about is books. I'm thinking next time you can drive up to San Antonio." He leaned closer and reached for her hand. "Maybe spend the night."

"We'll see," Remi said. She wanted to answer, "not in your wildest dreams," but she wasn't that bold.

Alana would have had no problem telling a date exactly what she thought of his inappropriate comments. Remi was more the type to simply count the minutes until she could get home and be done with the evening.

So much for giving another guy a chance. All this date had proved to her was that Linc was her type of guy. The kind of man who took his mother out for a nice dinner and spent his free time reading.

Alana had been urging Remi to try a dating app, and she almost laughed at the thought of her profile. "Bookish introvert seeks equally literary, dependable man who loves his mom and quiet nights reading next to each other on the sofa."

The average age of her matches would probably be eighty.

"Are you still with me?"

She blinked as Andrew waved a hand in front of her face. "Sorry," she said automatically. "I was just thinking."

"I hope you were thinking about what a great time you're having tonight. I sure am."

"That's good." She wondered if he'd pick up on her evasive answer.

Alas, no. Andrew went on to tell her another story about the wild world of financial analysts. Remi resisted the urge to lift her head and survey the room to see where Linc and his mother were sitting.

Books, she reminded herself. Book boyfriends were definitely better.

"I was surprised to see Remi on a date tonight," Kimberly said as she looked past Linc's shoulder a half hour later. "The man she's with doesn't seem like her type."

"At all," Linc agreed, his jaw clenched. "What in the world could she see in that d—" He cleared his throat. "That doofus."

"Perhaps she agreed to a date because he found the courage to ask her on one."

"He has to be the guy that Paul said was flirting with her at the store last weekend. Remi doesn't go on dates with random guys. Any guys."

"It's about time she did, then." Kimberly pointed her fork in his direction. "She's a pretty girl."

"She's gorgeous," Linc agreed. "Also smart and funny and kind."

"Then why does it surprise you that someone asked her out?" Kimberly inclined her head as she studied him.

"It doesn't surprise me that a guy asked. It surprises me that she said yes."

"Because you prefer her quietly pining after you?"

"Yea—" His eyes narrowed. "We're friends. She's not pining."

"She likes you, Linc."

He thumped the heel of his hand against his forehead. "Why is everyone suddenly trying to push Remi and me together?"

"Who's everyone?"

"You, Paul, Alec, and my Three-Stooges brothers." He shook his head. "I bet if I called Justine, she'd weigh in on it."

"Your sister is a smart lady. Your brothers and friends as well."

"Are you saying I'm not smart?"

"Linc." She reached for his hand and placed her smaller one over it. His mother's hands were tiny but strong. They'd seen a lot and worked more than they should have over the years. "You know what I'm saying."

"Remi isn't interested in me in that way."

His mom scoffed.

"I would know," he insisted.

"Lincoln, I love you. You are not only intelligent but also kind and hardworking, with an amazing sense of loyalty. I hesitate to say anything after how badly I messed up with your sister. I know I didn't do the best job as a mom. I was overwhelmed by having five little ones on my own."

"You did great, Mom. We all turned out great. The verdict's still out on Damon, but the rest of us function pretty well."

His mom smiled at the obvious joke. "I'm being serious, Linc. You had to take on too much for a young boy. I remember when your father left. I was scared out of my mind because I knew I was going to have another baby, and I could barely handle the four of you."

"It's a good thing Justine was a girl," he said with a grin, hoping to lighten his mother's mood. He didn't want to have this conversation and hated how wistful Kimberly became when they talked about the past.

His younger siblings had expected a lot from her, and some of the time she struggled to give them what they needed. Linc had never judged her for it, because he was old enough to know how hard it had been on her when Rick left.

He remembered hearing her cry in her bedroom at night when she thought he and his brothers were sleeping. He knew how exhausted raising the five of them made her and the toll it took on her body and spirit. He'd tried to step in wherever he could to help ease her burden and make things okay for his brothers and Justine.

Maybe if he'd tried sooner, his dad wouldn't have left. He shook his head. Just like when he and his brothers discussed Rick deserting his family, Linc knew there was no peace in second-guessing or playing the what-if game.

"You and Justine will continue to work things out," he assured his mother. "Your grandson adores you, and that will make it smoother."

She nodded and squeezed his fingers. "It already has. But you aren't going to distract me with talk of your sister. I'm not going to tell you what to do as far as your relationship with Remi goes. But I will say that you have a right to be happy. You're due some fun in your life."

"We drove over in the Ferrari. A sports car is the epitome of fun."

"I'm not talking about a car. I'm talking about companionship. Yes, it wasn't easy being a single parent. But the hardest part was missing your dad. He wasn't a perfect husband, but I loved him. I thought we loved each other."

Linc didn't know how to answer that. He'd thought his father had loved all of them, but Rick had left. He'd loved Christine, and she had left. Linc didn't trust love.

"I don't know how many times I have to say it. I'm not looking for a relationship or even sure I'm capable of falling in love. I would never do to a woman or children what Dad did to us. There's nothing that can make me change my mind."

"You aren't your father. Rick was greatly influenced by his experience with Wendell Fortune, or should I say lack of experience? It's not the same for you."

"I know," Linc answered. "It's worse. Wendell Fortune didn't want to be a father. My dad chose it multiple times and then left anyway. Our grandfather didn't know what he was missing. But there was no question Dad understood what he was leaving behind."

Kimberly's eyes filled with sadness. "I wish I could have done something to make him stay."

Linc smiled as the waiter approached their table with the calamari he'd ordered. This was the only restaurant in Chatelaine to serve the dish. He told himself he hadn't ordered it because it reminded him of his lunch with Remi.

Maybe she and her bachelor-party guy had shared a plate. He shook his head and focused on his mother as the waiter left. "No more talk about Rick Maloney. This is a night out for the two of us."

"I don't know that I've ever considered eating squid," she said with a wary look at the appetizer.

"You're going to love it, Mom. Plus, you'd better get used to indulging in the finer things on the regular. When Max, Coop and Damon get their money, you know we'll compete to see who spoils you the most."

The sadness in her eyes was replaced with affection and gratitude. "I'm lucky to have such amazing children."

"We're lucky to have you. I don't want you to worry about me. I'm happy. It would be crazy not to be, in my current situation."

She seemed to take him at his word, which was good. He made sure not to look over toward where Remi sat with her date for the rest of the meal. He was happy for his friend if she liked the guy.

As he told his mom, Linc had every reason in the world to be happy. Millions of them. In fact, he planned to concentrate more on enjoying his new life and not worry about missed opportunities. He'd had enough of regrets.

Chapter Eight

Remi turned a corner in the GreatStore stockroom the following Tuesday morning, only to find Paul and Alec with a couple of guys from the garden department huddled in a circle. Their heads were bent over Alec's phone, studying the device.

"You're supposed to play video games on your own time," she told them with a laugh, then noticed they all looked guilty. "Wait. Are you playing video games right now?"

Paul shook his head. "Not even a little. We're discussing serious business, Remi. Have you talked to Linc lately?"

She stopped and pressed a suddenly sweaty palm to her apron. Did Linc tell his friends about seeing her on the date? "I haven't. The last time Linc and I hung out was at the movie party. What's going on? Is there something wrong?"

The garden guys moved toward the back of the warehouse as Paul and Alec stepped toward her.

"Not wrong, exactly," Alec said. "But weird. Last night, we were over to watch a game, and he's gone full millionaire binge-shopper. The house is crowded with crap, which is totally unlike Lincoln Maloney."

Remi sucked in a breath and thought of the package she'd received yesterday when she got home from work, a signed first-edition Harry Potter hardcover in mint condition. There'd been no return address, just a note inside that simply said, "Hardcovers are special."

Even without Linc signing the note, she'd known the book was from him. No one else she knew would send a gift like that or have the means to access something so rare and unique.

The book confused Remi because now she didn't know what it meant. Listening to Paul and Alec talk about the random purchases Linc had made in the past few days made her feel like it wasn't special.

According to the two of them, he'd bought a pinball machine for Alec and given Paul a new set of golf clubs even though Paul didn't golf.

Apparently, four brand-new bikes that he'd ordered for his brothers were sitting in his living room. He'd sent Justine a kid-sized, battery-powered Ferrari for Morgan that matched Uncle Linc's sports car.

"I know he has a lot of money." Paul made a face.

"Not the exact amount, although I think it's more than I can probably imagine. But you've heard of lottery winners going bankrupt in a couple of years because they spend too much. They blow through a fortune."

Remi shook her head. "Linc *is* a Fortune. And he's smarter than that."

"He's not acting smart. He's acting…" Alec's mouth pulled tight like he didn't want to say what he was thinking.

Remi racked her brain, trying to think of what could be so horrible. Was he going to whisper that Linc had turned into a vampire or something equally bizarre?

"He's being irresponsible," Alec said in a harsh tone. "Linc is never irresponsible. He's like you in that way. That's why we thought you guys would make such a perfect pair."

Paul nodded. "It's true. We couldn't imagine a more perfect or boring couple than the two of you."

"Why do people keep calling Linc and me boring? We are not boring. I am not boring. I have a fascinating life." She stomped her foot when her two friends just stared at her. "Okay, I might not be exciting, but I'm not boring. Although I guess boring is better than irresponsible."

"We don't know what to do," Paul admitted.

"We need to stage an intervention," Alex suggested. "Do we call his brothers or his mom?"

Paul placed a heavy hand on Alec's shoulder. "It

would break Kimberly's heart to see him like this. She raised him better."

"Oh, for the love of—" Remi threw up her hands. "I'll go to his house after I get off work and talk to him. I need to thank him, anyway."

"Because he sent you something extravagant?" Paul leaned closer. "Was it perfume or a fancy designer purse? Spill it, Remi. What did you get?"

"A book."

"A book?" they chorused.

"Not just any book. A special book, a first edition."

"I don't even know what that means," Paul said. "But it gives me hope. If Linc thinks a book is a good gift, that means practical and boring Linc is still in there." He pointed at Remi. "You are just the practical, boring person to find him. You can do it, Remi. We believe in you."

"I'm going on break," she said through clenched teeth. "If either one of you calls me boring again, I'm going to go off in a way that shows you how not boring I can be."

"But you'll go see him," Paul confirmed.

"Was this whole thing a setup? A ruse to trap me into saying I'd go see him. You could have just asked."

"You went out with another guy last week," Alec said as if she might not remember. "We figured you might be taking a Linc hiatus."

"Linc and I are friends. It's not a big deal that I went on a date. I'll go see him and do my best to confirm he's doing okay."

Their apparent mission accomplished, Paul and Alec headed back to work. Remi had been on her way to the break room but stepped outside and took in a deep pull of fresh air instead.

She needed to clear her head as well as her heart and decide the best way to deal with Linc. She didn't like to think of him going off the rails or doing something so out of character, even if he could afford it. She also didn't want to admit how much it hurt that he was indiscriminately giving gifts.

The book had been the most precious present she'd ever received. A part of her had believed he'd sent it as a sign that the conversation he and his mom had with her and Andrew about books over dinner made Linc realize that the two of them were meant for something more. Remi tied her apron tighter and headed back to her shift.

Today, she was covering the book department and working backup in Electronics since the book customers had petered out, now that everyone who'd come in to ask her about Linc had found out she didn't know the amount of his inheritance.

It didn't take long for word to spread in a town like Chatelaine, which meant that people probably also knew that he was on a spending spree.

If it was making him happy, she wanted to ensure no one tried to worm their way into his life to take advantage of his generosity.

Paul and Alec might not take life seriously, but they were true friends. Linc's brothers would never take advantage of him either, not that they needed to since they would soon have their own money according to what Linc had told her.

Remi smiled at a mother who'd brought her daughter in to buy a set of sparkly headphones. She kept busy for the rest of the day and, when her shift was over, pointed her car in the direction of Linc's house.

She thought about getting the Harry Potter book first, possibly to return it to him. Would that be appropriate?

She didn't want to offend him. Plus, the book was precious to her. Both for what it meant and what it meant that he'd gifted it to her. Pulling to a stop in front of his house, she noticed his truck in the driveway, which meant the Ferrari must be tucked away in the garage.

She would have thought he'd leave it out during good weather for everybody to see. Although maybe that was unnecessary since nearly every Chatelaine resident already knew about Lincoln Fortune Maloney and his newfound wealth.

As she approached the house, she realized he didn't need the Ferrari in view as a sign of his changed status. There were boxes piled high on both sides of the tiny porch, and two pairs of skis sat against the wall along with what looked like an electric scooter and a fancy-looking grill.

She knew many Texans traveled to Colorado during the winter, but not many people in their town had the means for that. Maybe he was planning a trip now that he was without a job.

Paul and Alec had been right—at least about the level of his spending. She knocked on the door and pulled her hair out of the ponytail she wore almost every day at GreatStore. Did it look as limp and lifeless as it felt?

She should have stopped at home to freshen up and change into nicer clothes than her faded jeans and long-sleeve T-shirt. Maybe the Ferrari wasn't in the garage like she assumed. Perhaps Linc was out— even on a date. What did she know about his life?

Just as she was getting ready to retreat to her car, the door opened to reveal Linc standing on the other side.

His mouth dropped open at the sight of her. Then his eyes lit in a way that made Remi's heart slam against her chest.

How could he look at her like that and not have some feelings for her?

"Hey, Remi." He wore dark jeans and a white T-shirt, his feet bare.

Her stomach should not do somersaults at the sight of Lincoln's toes, but the sensation didn't exactly surprise her.

She knew how bad she had it, even if she wanted to deny her feelings. "Hey, Linc. I hope it's okay that I stopped by. I didn't see the Ferrari so I wasn't sure if you were home. If you're busy…"

He shook his head and gestured her inside. "The

car's in the garage, and it's great to see you. Did you just get off work?"

"I probably should have stopped home first. I look like I've had a long day, right?" She laughed even as she cursed herself on the inside. He probably thought she was fishing for a compliment.

"You look great," he said solemnly. "It's nice to see you. I would have cleaned up the house a bit if I'd known you were coming."

He gestured to the living room, which was also crowded with boxes and random merchandise.

"Big night on the Home Shopping Network?" she asked.

Linc massaged a hand across the back of his neck. "I bought a few things online. Maybe a couple of them were from the Home Shopping Network."

A laugh burst out of her mouth before she could stop it. "I was joking, Linc."

"They have nice merchandise featured in the late-night segments, and I haven't been sleeping well. I didn't mean to buy anything." He glanced around as if seeing the items for the first time. "I didn't mean to buy a lot of this stuff. It just happened."

"I came over to thank you for the book."

His shoulders relaxed. "Did you like it?"

"Of course I liked it. It was amazing and thought-ful. You didn't have to buy anything for me."

"Books are special to you, and I wanted to get you something."

"You bought gifts for a lot of people, according to Paul and Alec."

"You talked to the two of them?"

"I work with them. You might have left us behind, but we're still together. I talk to them on a regular basis."

"But you talk to them about *me*?"

"I would say they talked to *me* about *you*, to be honest. They're worried about your spending habits."

"I'm not going to blow through my money, and I haven't bought gifts for everyone—just my close friends. I've gotten things I thought would mean something. Paul has always wanted to join the LC Club. His parents got divorced when we were kids. His dad remarried and moved to San Antonio. Paul had a stepbrother who was our age. His dad belonged to the LC Club with his new family. Paul was invited during the summer, although he also worked there, making things awkward. His stepbrother had a real attitude problem. I don't know what the guy does now, but it was rough when we were in high school. I wanted to give Paul golf clubs and a membership to the club if he wants one. They say money can't buy happiness, and I guess that's true. But it can make life easier and give you opportunities you wouldn't have without it or books you wouldn't be able to afford on your own."

Remi sighed. She'd known something was going on with Linc, an edginess to him. But the story proved what Paul had told them. The Linc they knew was still in there.

He might have money or be struggling with adjusting to his new life, but that didn't change who he was.

"So what are you going to do with all this stuff? Is that a pogo stick?"

"I was watching the late-night exercise show, and the guy was using a pogo stick to work out. I have a lot of time on my hands."

"I think a gym membership might serve you better."

"Probably," he agreed with a laugh.

She liked making him laugh.

Linc glanced around his home and tried to see the piles of merchandise through Remi's eyes. It didn't reflect well that he still wasn't sure what had possessed him to go on a shopping spree over the past week.

Other than seeing Paul and Alec, he'd been alone in his house ordering expedited shipping on items from kitchen gadgets to sporting equipment to home decor he didn't need or truly want. What was he trying to prove?

Everyone knew he was wealthy, and the myriad of purchases certainly didn't make a difference in how he felt about himself or his situation.

"I have to admit seeing all of this through your eyes makes me feel like a fool for buying most of it."

"I never want to make you feel that way," Remi told him. "It's your money. You can do whatever you want with it."

He wanted to get rid of the hollow feeling in his stomach but didn't say it out loud. Poor little rich guy. No one would feel sorry for him, nor did he want that.

"I'll find a good use for the purchases. I might donate some of it."

She looked like she was trying to hide a smile. "I'm sure there are plenty of less fortunate people in Chatelaine who would love a new pair of skis."

"Okay, the skis were dumb, but check out my back massager." He gestured to a chair sitting in the corner of the room. It was a black leather monstrosity with at least a dozen different settings and a heating and cooling function. Top of the line.

"That thing looks like something you'd find on a spaceship."

"Have a seat."

She shook her head. "I really shouldn't."

"Come on, Rem," he coaxed. "I remember long shifts on the floor at GreatStore."

She laughed and rolled her eyes. "It's only been a few weeks since you were a working stiff like the rest of us. I hope you remember."

"Exactly," he told her. "Which is why I want you to try it."

She still looked dubious but moved toward the oversize chair.

He hadn't felt a damn thing when the items he'd purchased had begun arriving, which had led him to buy more. Even though he was embarrassed by the extravagance, sharing them with Remi made happiness bloom inside his chest. He tried to tamp down the emotions swirling through him.

He'd seen her out on a date after all. It was more than likely he'd missed his chance, but he still wasn't sure he wanted a real shot with her.

As much as he enjoyed hanging out with Remi, he couldn't lie to himself. His feelings for her weren't casual. Linc feared it would turn into something out of his control if he let himself get close.

He wouldn't—couldn't—lose control, afraid that he took after Rick Maloney and possibly Wendell Fortune. His heart wasn't made for love or commitment.

He didn't believe that the guy he'd seen Remi with could make her happy. But who was he to judge when he wasn't sure about himself either?

He grabbed the remote off the coffee table as she lowered herself into the massage chair.

"Do I strap in and blast off now?" She laughed as he hit the button for the remote and adjusted the settings.

"Oh." Her dark eyes went wide.

"It's nice, right?"

"It's...different." Her breath caught slightly.

"Try to relax. Tell me when it's the right speed."

She nodded and closed her eyes as he fiddled with the controls.

"That's good," she said about midway through the levels. He switched the setting to a gentle pulse and enjoyed the sight of her settling in more deeply.

"It's very nice," she admitted. "This was a good purchase."

"I thought so. Money might not buy happiness," he said, "but it can give you a good massage. Can I get you a beer or something to drink?"

"A glass of water, but I don't want to put you out."

"I'm happy you're here."

He returned with a water for her and a beer for himself but paused in the doorway to admire her for a few seconds. Her eyes remain closed. It looked like she might have fallen asleep in the chair. Her head tipped slightly to one side, and her breathing seemed to have slowed.

She looked peaceful and relaxed. When was the last time he'd watched a woman sleep? Linc was more out of practice dating than he realized. Even when he'd been with a woman in the past few years, it hadn't been all night.

He'd accepted his boundaries but could imagine Remi in his bed with her hair fanned out around her and her scent surrounding him. His body tightened in response to the image.

He shook his head because as quickly as the glorious image entered his brain, he remembered that she was more likely to be sleeping with another guy. One who was smart enough to make her his.

Linc rarely considered himself stupid, but his worries about what he could and couldn't give in a relationship were just that.

Paul and Alec had been right all along, which was also difficult to admit. He liked Remi as more than a friend and wanted her to be more than a friend. There was no point in continuing to deny it.

It didn't have to mean something more. Linc would make his parameters clear. She was a reasonable woman who could appreciate that and decide with all the facts at hand.

He reminded himself what those parameters were because his body and heart seemed to want to short-circuit his brain every time she was near him.

She blinked and glanced around, her gaze almost sensually soft. Then their eyes locked, and she quickly sat up. "I fell asleep."

At the way her cheeks turned pink, Linc wondered if his wanton thoughts were obvious when she looked at him. The last thing he wanted to do was cause her distress. "I'm glad to offer you a few minutes of rest. As far as I'm concerned, the massage chair is a winner."

"I didn't mean to make you feel bad about buying things." She took the glass of water, his skin tingling with electricity when their fingers brushed. "Just remember it's not all about possessions. Your wealth can open the door to all kinds of experiences, maybe even a vacation. You haven't been on one since I've known you, Linc."

"You're right." He sipped his beer. "Although I'm not sure how to start planning. Where would you go?"

"I don't know," she told him, shaking her head. "There are so many places I haven't been. I wouldn't know how to begin to choose."

"Then let me pick," he suggested on a whim. "I like what you said about using my money for experiences. I want to experience something new with you. Are you off this weekend?"

Remi nodded, looking dumbfounded, so Linc plunged forward. "Go away with me…" Her big eyes widened even more. "Separate rooms, of course," he said, then wanted to kick himself for making the invitation awkward.

Something that looked like disappointment flashed in her eyes, shocking him. Was it possible she might want a different arrangement?

"Where would we go?"

"It's a surprise." It would be a surprise to both of them since he needed to figure it out. The thought of a weekend away with Remi shouldn't send his heart into overdrive. They were friends. It was like going away with Paul and Alec or his brothers, except it was nothing like that.

"What should I pack?"

"You'll go with me?"

She grinned. "Yes, it sounds amazing. I'm certain whatever you have planned will be amazing."

"Amazing," he repeated. No pressure. "Pack for warm weather," he told her as an idea formed in his mind. "Plus good walking shoes and a bathing suit."

"Okay." She giggled. "I'm not sure I'm influencing you the way Paul and Alec expected. I was supposed to make you remember your practical side."

"I haven't forgotten, but that doesn't mean we can't have a little fun." His idea of fun was splashing in the ocean with Remi in a bikini, her bare legs wrapped around him in the water. He shook his head to clear the sexy image. They were friends. His mind could remember that even if his body seemed to forget at every turn.

Chapter Nine

"This is the most fun I've ever had in my life." Remi swayed closer to Linc as they walked down the crowded Santa Monica Pier three days later.

She still could hardly believe how perfect their impromptu getaway had been so far.

The weekend had started with Linc chartering a private jet, which felt so extravagant that she'd almost refused to climb on board. He'd explained it was already paid for, so if they didn't use it the money would go to waste.

It had been such a thrill, and she'd felt like a celebrity exiting the plane under the California sun a few hours later.

Linc had thought of everything, from a boutique hotel overlooking the water to a private tour at her dream amusement park. He'd even bought her a custom wand, which she would treasure forever as a memento of their time together.

She couldn't allow herself to think it would last, although Linc freely talked about other adventures he saw in the future. Enough that Remi almost believed that future might include her.

She should know better than to read too much into it, but there was no denying she was falling for him even more than when they'd worked together.

In the past, her feelings had best been described as a crush. Now, between the car-buying expedition and this trip, she was getting to know Linc at a deeper level. The more she learned about him, the more her feelings grew.

She wouldn't say the word *love* out loud because she didn't want to take the chance on scaring him or ruining this happy moment. But her heart was filled with love, and she held it close like a precious gift.

After closing down the amusement park yesterday, they'd returned to the hotel where, as promised, they had separate bedrooms in the suite he'd reserved, much to her chagrin.

She'd woken this morning disappointed to be alone but thrilled at the thought of another full day discovering southern California with Linc.

They'd driven up the coast and walked along the beach. Although the water had been too cold to consider swimming, Remi loved dipping her toes in the surf. She loved everything about being with him.

"You were right about splurging on experiences.

This is way better than buying random stuff," Linc told her as they continued toward the restaurant.

The sun dipped low in the western sky, painting the horizon in shades of orange and pink. Remi wasn't sure she'd ever seen anything more beautiful.

"I think this experience was so great because it's with you," she answered with a contented smile. "Although the wand kind of tipped it over the edge of perfect, so maybe we won't rule out the value of purchases just yet. It's nice when they mean something, like the book you gave me or Paul's golf clubs." She squeezed his arm. "You might want to explain their significance to him."

"Good point," Linc conceded. "I don't think he's considered that he has as much right to belong to the club as anyone else. I want him to believe that."

The hotel concierge had made reservations for them at an exclusive and intimate restaurant overlooking the ocean. The interior was contemporary in design with clean lines and a neutral color palette that made the surrounding landscape the star of the show. There was a bar with a backlit stone slab as its base and beautiful copper chandeliers throughout.

The hostess escorted them to a table with the most amazing view of the sea and the nearby pier. Remi gazed around at the other patrons, several of whom were staring at the couple who'd been shown to such a prime spot.

She knew people must think they were something special and suddenly wished she possessed Alana's style and self-confidence. Linc should have someone on his arm who could not only appreciate the means he had, but also fit in with his new station in life.

"What's wrong?" He leaned forward across the gorgeously set table. "Don't you like it?"

"It's lovely." Remi did her best to arrange her features into a more pleasant expression. "I was thinking that all these potential new experiences are bound to take you far from Chatelaine. Your life is going to be much bigger than it was before. I'll miss you when that happens," she told him honestly.

To her disappointment, he didn't deny her assessment of the situation. "I never dreamed of the possibility of leaving Chatelaine. I have to figure out if it's the home I would choose now that I have a choice. I can't keep hanging around GreatStore like some kind of big-box store stalker. People are going to get sick of seeing my face when they're at work."

Remi bit down on her lip to keep from responding. She would never get sick of seeing Linc, but she wouldn't hold him back.

Her gaze wandered toward the waves crashing as the sun ducked behind the horizon. "You've got the whole world at your fingertips," she reminded him. "You can do anything or be anything you want."

The waiter approached the table and took their drink orders. A glass of white wine for Remi and a beer for Linc. She smiled to herself at the automatic comparison to Andrew and his fancy bourbon and giant ice cube. Being with Linc was better in every way.

"I want a purpose," he said, also gazing out to the ocean.

"That's noble."

He looked at her warily.

"You don't believe me?"

"You're a good guy, Linc. Of course you want your life to have purpose. I think we all want that."

He sighed audibly and took a long pull on his beer when the waiter brought it. She didn't like the interruptions because she wanted to hear what Linc had to say.

There were deep facets to him she wanted to explore while she had the chance.

The waiter recommended a special tasting menu the restaurant offered, paired with a glass of wine for each course. Linc seemed as relieved as Remi to have some of the decision-making taken out of his hands.

She hadn't thought about the pressure he must feel now that he'd received his inheritance, but it clearly weighed on him. "I told my brothers about wanting a purpose, and they thought I was being ridiculous. Spending my money should be enough of a purpose, they said."

She wrinkled her nose. "I think you've proven in the past week that's not the case."

"True, and I downloaded the syllabus for my new business class. It starts next week. It feels strange to go back to school, especially in a program with people so much younger than me. I'm excited about learning the different aspects of running a business. It's the part of my job at GreatStore that I miss the most. Maybe now I can find something that belongs to me."

She nodded. "Own the company, be your own boss."

"Have a purpose," they said at the same time and both smiled. The first course came, and Remi allowed herself to relax for the rest of the evening. She wanted Linc to enjoy it as much as she did.

If she could give him that this weekend, it might in some way pay him back for treating her to such a special time, although she knew he didn't want or expect payback.

He was generous and took as much pleasure in her excitement and enjoyment as he did in his own. She wished he could see himself the way she saw him.

There was more to him than the man who'd given up whatever dreams he'd had to take care of his mom and siblings. Linc might try to downplay it, but he had one of the kindest hearts of any person she knew. He was a natural leader, and the staff at GreatStore instinctively looked to him for answers to any challenges that arose.

He didn't back down from doing what he thought was right and had a fiercely protective side. Although she knew he'd never falter under the weight of his responsibilities, this time away was a chance for both of them to let go a bit. She wanted him to see that he was as safe with her as she felt with him.

As the dinner continued, they talked about topics ranging from their childhoods to books to lists of their respective favorite things.

She laughed as he told her about some of the shenanigans he and his brothers had gotten into when they were kids. The longer the night went on, the more animated Linc became and the harder she fell for him.

She told herself that even though it would be hard when he inevitably moved on to someone more suited to the man he was now, any heartbreak she felt was bound to be worth it.

Remi had never been much of an adventurer, but this was her chance to be the heroine of her own story, even though it might be over too soon, just like in her favorite books. But this was better than any make-believe story because Linc was next to her. This was real life, and despite her fear, she wanted to make the most of it.

Every few steps, his hand brushed her, sending a cascade of sparks along her skin. Could he feel the electricity between them? She could see the shadow of stubble on his jaw and wanted to lift her hand and cradle his face in her palms. She wanted to kiss him…she wanted more than kisses, even if it wasn't forever.

She'd have the memories to enjoy in the coming years, but only if she was bold enough to reach for what she wanted. What she'd always wanted was Linc.

They walked back on the beach; the night sky was filled with a canopy of stars. It had grown so dark that it was difficult to see past the ocean, but the sound of the rolling waves was constant and comforting.

He started to turn in the direction of the hotel, but she tugged on his hand. Be brave, she told herself, anxious but unwilling to let this chance pass her by. "Linc, wait. I'm not ready to go back yet."

"Is everything okay?"

Her heart flipped over again, and she focused her gaze on his full mouth because it was too difficult to look him in the eyes and say what she needed to. Her body felt flooded with warmth and her hands tingled with the need to touch him.

"I'm not ready…"

"You don't have to be, Remi. There's no pressure for—"

She lifted a finger to his mouth. "I don't want this night to end," she said on a rush of breath. "I want to be with you…to be together. I want you to make love to me, Linc."

He didn't answer for a moment, and she wondered if she'd shocked him—hopefully he wasn't horrified by her words.

It was still too much to look directly into his eyes as her face flamed with embarrassment. Just when she was about to turn tail and run, he grabbed her hand that still rested on his mouth.

He linked their fingers and leaned in to kiss her, teasing her lips with his. His mouth was warm and spicy with the subtle hint of the wine they'd shared at dinner. It was everything she'd ever dreamed and more. Linc kissed her like he already knew every one of her secret desires, the kind of lustful thoughts Remi was embarrassed to think.

But not with him. The way he savored her made her feel brave. She wanted to be a woman who could handle a kiss like this. A woman who would revel in whatever sexy demands Linc made.

Remi felt intoxicated by the contact and wondered how much better things could get between them. His kiss was worth risking her heart and to finally discover the courage to live, and not just read about desire and adventures on the pages of a book.

She wanted to be the heroine of her own story.

"Look at me," he said when he pulled away a few moments later, his hand moving around the back of her neck, stroking the tense muscles there.

She swallowed and forced her gaze to meet his. His green eyes had softened like a grassy meadow in the morning mist. Desire swirled in their depths, and an answering yearning hummed through her.

"Remi, I want to make love to you tonight," he said solemnly like she was precious. Like he meant those words to his very soul. "Are you certain that's what you want, too?"

Remi had never felt anything like the sensations swirling through her body, and that was just from his words and his fingers massaging her neck. She couldn't imagine how much truly being with him would affect her.

But she wanted to know. She'd spent too long guarding her heart. This was her chance with Linc, and she wasn't going to waste it.

"More than anything," she told him honestly.

He dropped another intense kiss on her lips, then squeezed her hand and started in the direction of the hotel. She had to practically jog to keep up with his long paces and would have laughed at his eagerness if it hadn't meant so much to her heart.

To her confidence.

When they were back in the suite, he led her to the bed in her room.

"Are you sure?" he asked as he took a step back from her.

She nodded.

"Thank God," he breathed and quickly began to undress. She was fascinated by the way his muscles bunched as he stripped out of his shirt and pants.

She tried not to gape. After all, his wasn't the first chest she'd ever seen. Except Linc's chest had played a starring role in most of her secret fantasies for as long as she could remember. And the reality of it seemed to short-circuit her good sense. There was no need for good sense right now.

With a small, sexy smile like he understood his effect on her, Linc reached out and his movements slowed.

He unzipped her dress with care, kissing his way down her spine as he pushed the fabric off her shoulders. Remi ran her hands over his smooth skin, absolutely blown away that he was hers to touch, at least for tonight. The sensation was so overwhelming, it felt like her knees might give way, but Linc was there to hold her steady.

When he lowered her to the bed and the heat of him enveloped her, she forgot all about her doubts and worries. This was right. It couldn't be anything but perfect between them. He knew her, and his wicked mouth and skilled hands moved over her, bringing her to the edge of losing all control.

"You are amazing," he said against the curve of her breast, slowly pushing her bra and then her panties down her body. He pressed heated kisses against her belly causing goose bumps to shiver along her spine.

Suddenly, Remi forgot to be nervous or embarrassed about her lack of experience. She felt amazing. She felt worthy and confident and so many things Remi had never associated with herself.

It gave her the courage to touch him the way she'd always wanted to, like he belonged to her. His skin was hot under her hands, and he groaned with pleasure when she grazed her fingernails along the hard planes of his back. There was no telling when or if this would happen again, so she was determined to make the most of every single moment.

After they'd spent what felt like hours discovering how the other liked to be touched and tasted, he rolled a condom over his length and entered her. It was everything she'd hoped for and more.

More than just him filling her in the most incredible way. He continued to kiss and stroke, coaxing her to delicious new heights of sensation. They moved together in a perfect rhythm, slow and seductive until she was panting underneath him. As Remi finally gave in to her release, she knew with every certainty that she would always belong to this man.

Chapter Ten

Linc was staring at the ocean waves the following morning when he heard the door to Remi's bedroom open. He'd been sitting in the lounge chair on the balcony in almost the same position since before sunrise, paralyzed with fear and guilt and a yearning for something he knew was beyond his reach.

Last night was the reason he hadn't had a serious relationship since Christine broke his heart. Casual sex was as much commitment as he could handle. He liked the women he dated, but he hadn't cared about them.

Not the way he did about Remi. Even though their night together had been more than he ever could have expected, his brokenness was going to ruin everything.

"Morning," she said, pulling her hair back into a low ponytail as she approached him.

"Hey." He inclined his head toward the tray he'd ordered from room service. "There's coffee and muffins if you want them now, plus brunch in the hotel restaurant so we can go down later."

She nodded. "You got up early."

"It's not too often I get to watch the rising sun play along the ocean waves."

"I wish you'd woken me," she said as she slipped into the chair next to him. "I could have watched it with you."

He'd been tempted when ribbons of pink and purple began to curl across the sky. Linc had been bowled over by the beauty of it.

Remi would have added to his enjoyment of the moment, but he hadn't woken her because that would reveal something he wasn't ready to admit, even to himself.

"I figured you'd like a chance to sleep in. I know how trying those early shifts at GreatStore can be. I don't have any reason to get up at the crack of dawn anymore, other than to watch the sunrise."

"That seems like reason enough," she said, pouring a cup of coffee.

"Anyway, we've got some time before the flight is scheduled to take us back. If you want to go shopping or—"

"Did I do something wrong?"

He turned to face her, saw the china mug held so

tightly between her hands he was surprised it didn't shatter.

"Why would you think that? Of course not."

"I mean, last night…" She kept her gaze focused on the table instead of making eye contact with him. Her cheeks had gone a bright shade of pink.

"It's been a while since…" Remi rolled her lips together. "You know, I thought it was good for both of us, but if not, well, for me—"

"It was perfect. You were perfect." He reached across the table and removed the cup from her hands, lacing their fingers together instead. The last thing he'd wanted to do was allow his fears and doubt to affect her.

"I had the most amazing time this weekend, and last night was beyond fantastic."

"I don't understand," she said, "why you're out here and the sheets on your side of the bed are cold."

"Like I said, I came out to watch the sunrise. It had nothing to do with you."

She scowled at him. "But there must be a reason. You don't have to pretend to spare my feelings. Like you said, this weekend has been amazing. I'll never forget it but—"

"I feel guilty," he blurted.

"Guilty? What did you do?"

Her tone had changed from wary to worried, and he wasn't sure which was worse. "I didn't do anything. That's the problem."

She smiled with a mischievous twinkle in her

eyes. "I remember you doing quite a few things that were pretty fantastic."

Linc laughed despite his troubled emotions. It was a credit to Remi that she could make him smile even in a situation like this.

"I feel guilty because I haven't done anything to deserve the way my life is right now. I'm the only one in my family who has the money, but my brothers won't let me take care of them."

"Their time will come," she reminded him.

"We hope so, but is there any guarantee? What would have happened if this money had been in the picture before my dad left? The four of us agree it probably wouldn't have changed anything, but we don't know for sure. What if he'd stayed?"

"You can't know, and it doesn't have anything to do with you. Why is your dad with us on this trip, Linc?"

He shook his head. "I don't know. I've had such a good weekend, but I can't let myself enjoy it. It's not just the money, Remi. That's a sorry excuse. We've been friends for a long time."

"Six years," she murmured, her eyes soft and wistful.

"So what if the timing is wrong? Everything is changing because of the money, but I don't feel changed. I've always been told that I look like my dad, and I've always been terrified of turning out like him. He hurt my mom deeply. He hurt all of us. I would never want to hurt you."

She frowned and he wouldn't blame her if she got

up and stomped away. "Life is full of risks, Linc. Neither of us has much experience taking them, but that doesn't mean we can't manage it."

"I don't want to ruin this weekend, Rem. What the hell is wrong with me that I can't just enjoy an amazing night with a beautiful woman?"

"There's nothing wrong other than your struggle to give yourself a break. You don't have to take me or any of your friends or family on lavish trips or buy us expensive gifts. There is nothing you need to do to deserve this bounty you've been given."

"That's the problem. I don't know how to function without needing to do something. Ever since my dad walked out on us, I've been working in some capacity. First, helping my mom with my siblings and then odd jobs around the neighborhood to bring in money. And then my career at GreatStore. Maybe quitting was a hasty decision, but it was my opportunity to do something more. I just don't know what that is. I'm a person who needs a purpose What purpose do I have now? I want to do nice things for the people in my life. I want to take care of people. That's what I do. Even that feels tainted by this money. I feel guilty because it's so easy. You've had a great weekend. But that's not because of me. It's because of the money. If the only way I can add value is by spending money on people, I don't think that says anything positive about me."

"It's not true. I had a great time this weekend because we are together." She squeezed his hand

and drew his attention, which had drifted out to the ocean. "You need to understand something. My reaction, whether it's to an amusement park or a sunrise, is not your responsibility, Linc. You can't control everything."

"I've always been in control. It's the only thing I know." He ran his free hand through his hair as he sighed. "The inheritance is messing with me. It feels ridiculous to complain, but I'm at loose ends. I don't know what to do about it." The words sounded pathetic even to his own ears. She was going to think he was the biggest baby she'd ever met. Who complained about having too much money? He felt ridiculous and wished he could take back all of it.

He'd broached the subject of his feelings about the inheritance with his brothers but nothing like how open and honest he was being with Remi. "Forget I said anything," he told her, releasing her hand and downing the last of his coffee. "Let's go get breakfast before we head to the airport. I remember from our breakfast staff meetings that you're a fan of pancakes."

She stood with him but stepped in front of him, her gaze direct as she inclined her head. "Lincoln Fortune Maloney, you're a good man. You were a good man before you were rich. Now that you're wealthy beyond belief, you're still a good man, just one who can afford to charter a plane. You don't always have to be the responsible one. I don't know what your father would have done if he'd received the inheritance when he was still married to your mom. But in some ways, it doesn't matter. You are the man you are because of how you had to step up. It might not be fair, but you took care of the people in your life. You still do." She threaded her fingers with his. "You don't always have to be the one taking care of other people." She rose up on tiptoe and brushed her mouth at the edge of his jaw. "Because sometimes," she said as her lips grazed his cheek, then whispered against his mouth, "it's okay to let another person take the lead."

"Is that what you're doing?"

"Yes." Her hands moved under his T-shirt and up the bare skin of his back, leaving a trail of heat in their wake. He knew all too well how clever she could be with those hands. "I'd like to," she said against his mouth. "If you'll let me."

"I can't honestly think of anything else I'd rather have happen at the moment."

She smiled and tugged him forward. "Relax, Linc. Just for a little while. I promise you'll like it."

His body hummed to life as he followed her through the suite to her bedroom. She looked so pleased with herself, with that sexy half smile and the uninhibited desire radiating in her sweet gaze.

His chest swelled, and he wanted to savor every moment of this weekend, to keep the real world out for as long as possible. They might not have much longer, but it was time enough to make sure they made the kind of memories together that would last a very long time.

* * *

"Sweetheart, I haven't seen you smile like this since your daddy built you that dollhouse for your tenth birthday. I don't think you could wipe the grin off your face if you tried."

Remi pursed her lips as she glanced at her mother sitting next to her at the counter of Chatelaine's Tumbleweed Diner. She also felt her mouth twitch at the edges. "It's been a good week," she said. "Sales were up in my department by almost twenty percent thanks to the new movie that just came out based on that book series. Although—"

"I know." Stella held up a hand. "Books are always better than the movie version. I don't think that's the only reason." She pointed at Remi. "You're grinning again."

"It's the pancakes," Remi said, shrugging. "Pancakes make me happy. Did I tell you about the pancakes we had at the hotel? They were as light as cotton candy, Mom."

"You told me about that and riding the Ferris wheel on the boardwalk and the private tour guide at the amusement park. It sounds like quite the weekend away for two young people."

"It was amazing," Remi agreed, then quickly added, "but we're just friends."

Her mother lifted a brow. "You keep saying that. It's almost like you're trying to convince yourself more than you're trying to convince me."

Remi bit down on her lower lip. She didn't like lying to her mother. She knew that Stella had a romantic heart. If she had any idea what had transpired between Remi and Linc, she'd be picking out wedding dresses before too long.

"I'm just saying he picked you to go on the trip, and I'm sure there were plenty of *friends*—" her mom made exaggerated air quotes around that last word "—who would have been happy to join him. I'm also saying that Linc might be the reason for your smile, not book sales."

"I love my job," Remi said primly.

"Sweetheart, you have to know when to fold them. I'm your mama, and I can read your game face like it's my job. It has been my job for a lot of years."

Stella glanced at the watch encircling her wrist. "I've got to get back to the office."

"Thanks for meeting me for lunch, Mom. I'll see you later tonight." Remi hugged her mother and then took another forkful of pancake as Stella walked away. "So good and needs more syrup," she murmured to herself and grabbed the little jar on the counter.

"Pancakes for lunch. That's an interesting selection," a voice said next to her. She turned to see an older man with a gray beard and a bulky cable-knit sweater, making himself more comfortable on the stool next to her.

"It's an acquired taste, but if you're looking for the perfect mix of carbs and sugar, you can't go wrong."

"I didn't know there was a perfect mix. I hope you don't mind that I overheard you and your mother's conversation."

"I don't mind," Remi said. "I'd like to believe there are secrets in Chatelaine, but I don't know anyone who can keep one."

The man seemed to consider that.

"You're not from around here, are you?" she asked him. She hadn't seen him before and figured she knew most of the residents of Chatelaine.

"Not exactly. My name's Martin."

She shook his outstretched hand. "Hello, Martin. I'm Remi."

"So you have a young man who's caught your fancy?"

"Getting to the heart of the matter, aren't we?"

"As I said, you're going to have to forgive an old man the curiosity. My life doesn't get all that exciting anymore, so I like to live vicariously. I enjoy meeting people with interesting stories."

Remi laughed and placed the syrup jar back on the counter. "Then you've come to the wrong place. Unfortunately, I'm about as dull as they come. Pancakes for lunch is my form of excitement."

"I thought I heard you say something about a private plane."

"That's true, but I was also living vicariously through a friend. He treated me to a weekend in California."

"A boyfriend?" Martin asked.

Remi laughed again, surprised at how comfortable she felt with her new friend, who was a veritable stranger. Except he didn't feel like a stranger.

Maybe that was Martin or maybe it was the Chatelaine effect. People in this town were curious and friendly, which made it easy to open up, even with a man she'd just met. "Remind me to keep you away from my mother, sir. Not a boyfriend. He's a fine man, and any woman would be lucky to have him."

"But he took you away for the weekend as friends?"

"It's complicated."

"The best stories always are."

The waitress came at that moment. With a wink at Remi, Martin ordered pancakes with a side of fries.

"Look at you being all extra," Remi told the older man with a laugh.

"It's about time I started doing what makes me happy in my life. If you tell me a bit more about your friend who's not a boyfriend, I'll share my fries."

"You drive a hard bargain." Remi placed her fork on the counter and dabbed at one corner of her mouth with a napkin. "What the heck? Maybe you'll have some fresh insight." She glanced around to make sure no one who worked at the restaurant or the patrons around them were listening. The last thing she needed was details of her relationship with Linc to be spread around town. More than enough tongues were already wagging. "My friend and I," she told Martin, careful not to mention Linc's name in case the older man ran into him, "have been friends for years, but…"

"You want something more," Martin guessed. "What's stopping that from happening?"

She shrugged. "He's never seen me that way. I didn't want to jeopardize our friendship by making things awkward. Up until a couple of weeks ago, we worked together."

"He changed jobs?"

"He came into some money—a lot of money. He quit the store where we worked, and he's trying to figure out what's next. The money has made him…"

"Not the man you fell for in the first place?"

She smiled. "You must be a fan of soap operas because you're adding more drama than is truly a part of the story. He's still a great guy. I think the money is going to be a blessing. For his whole life, my friend has been shackled with too much responsibility, commitments, and taking care of people in ways that weren't his choice. Now he has the financial means to take care of the people in his life and still live his best life."

She sighed. "With the whole world at his fingertips, I don't know why he would choose me."

"It sounds like he did choose you for the weekend."

She breathed in a deep, calming breath. "He did. Thank you for that reminder."

The pancakes and french fries arrived. Martin handed Remi the ketchup bottle that sat on the counter and then drenched his pancakes in syrup before scooping up a large forkful. He held it up in mock salute and smiled at her. "I think anyone adventurous enough to order pancakes for lunch is a woman worth knowing. It sounds like your friend realizes that." He waggled his brows as he chewed the pancake. "If the money hasn't corrupted him, is his family pressuring him?" he continued as he ate.

She shook her head. "His three brothers and sister are also supposed to inherit, but he's taking care of them until that happens. As I said, he's a fine man. He's happy to take care of people."

The older man's hunched shoulders seemed to straighten, as if Remi's description of Linc relieved Martin of some unseen burden.

"Are you visiting family in Chatelaine?" she asked, suddenly curious about the man who seemed so interested in her life.

"Yes, I'm here to look in on my family, but I think I'm going to have a hard time topping this lunch." He ate another forkful of pancakes.

She laughed. "You're a charmer, Martin. You remind me a bit of my friend."

The look of shock on the older man's face was hilarious, and he brushed his thumb against the corner of his eye. "That's the nicest thing anybody has said to or about me in a while. If your friend is half the man you think him to be, he'll see what a prize you are. Money might buy him a lot of things, but love isn't one of them. And at the end of the day, it's the only thing that really matters."

Remi reached out and squeezed his arm. "That's the nicest thing I've heard in a long time as well. Now, let's enjoy our pancake lunch."

Chapter Eleven

"If you're not going to drive it, you could at least loan it to me to take out for a spin."

"Not a chance." Linc shook his head as he turned from loading the back of his truck and stared at his brother. "Damon, hand me another one of those boxes."

"What is all this stuff, bro?"

"Donations."

"You're donating a brand-new set of pots and pans?" he asked as he looked at the box he'd picked up. "Why do you even have new cookware? You don't cook with your new pots, and you don't drive your new car. What's going on?"

"I do drive the car, but I need the truck to take this stuff to the Community Fund Thrift Store. Since all proceeds from the merchandise they sell go to the

Chatelaine Fund and help the community, I figured I'd give them some things I don't need."

"Like the car you don't drive?" Damon insisted as he handed over the box. "Donate that to me."

"Why won't you believe me? I drive it. I'm just not driving it at the moment."

"Can I borrow it?"

"No. Wait your turn and buy your own car."

"Would you let Remi drive it?"

Linc paused in the process of loading a box of bedding, most of the items with the tags still on, into the truck's bed. If he'd known his brother would be stopping by, he wouldn't have chosen right now to empty his house.

He could easily have returned most of this stuff he'd bought unnecessarily, but he'd chosen not to. He figured at least his rash behavior could benefit people who needed it.

He'd also scheduled a meeting with the director of the Chatelaine Fund to talk about how else he could make an impact locally.

Maybe philanthropy would give him the feeling of purpose still lacking from his life. He hated the emptiness that seemed to be consuming him. He didn't feel it when he was with Remi, which was a different kind of challenge. He'd stopped into Great-Store a couple of times since their California trip, but it was hard to spend quality time with her there.

They'd had lunch together twice, and he'd asked her out to dinner, but she'd made an excuse about needing to spend time with her mother. It seemed as though Linc wasn't the only one on shaky ground since the trip.

Every time he walked into the store, he felt like his friends and former coworkers were staring at him—at the two of them. After their night together in California, Linc was worried his feelings would be written all over his face. He couldn't reveal them until he understood how Remi felt. Until he knew he wouldn't hurt her. That was the last thing he wanted.

"Remi doesn't want to drive my car," he told his brother as they placed the last boxes in the truck.

"Not even your stick shift?" Damon laughed at his own dumb joke.

"I'm going to hurt you," Linc said without missing a beat. "One more comment like that, and you're going down."

"It was a joke. I was kidding."

"It's not funny."

"Lighten up, Linc. It's obvious you like her."

"We've been friends for years."

"Are you seriously still feeding yourself that tired line?"

"It's not a line." Linc shook his head. "It's a fact."

"As much of a fact as you acting like a fool?" Damon demand. "You took her away for the weekend on a private plane. That's not a casual invitation."

"How do you know about that?" Linc's eyes narrowed. "Has Remi been talking about our weekend? What is she saying?"

"I wasn't aware your trip was some *Mission Impossible* deal that needed to be kept top secret. If so, you shouldn't have flown out of the regional airport. I have no idea who Remi has talked to or what she's said. I didn't hear anything from her. She doesn't seem like the type to kiss and tell. Anyway, my source isn't important. Why does it have to be such a state secret?"

Link studied his brother warily. "I never said we kissed."

"True." Damon rolled his eyes. "I guess I assumed that because I didn't think you were a complete idiot. What good is Wendell Fortune's money if it doesn't help you land a hot chick?"

"It's a wonder you're so popular with the ladies when you say things like 'hot chick.' Tell me more of your secrets, master."

Damon laughed and ambled toward the passenger side of Linc's truck. "It's my natural charm," he said as they climbed in. "You wouldn't understand."

"I don't need company on this errand," Linc told his brother as he gave him the side-eye.

"You need more than company. You need somebody to shake some sense into you."

Linc shoved a pair of sunglasses onto the bridge of his nose, grateful for the protection they offered from his brother's too-knowing gaze. "Do you truly believe that?"

"Don't you? If not, how do you explain the deal with Remi?"

"Maybe her feelings for me have changed because of the money. If there's something more between us…" He took one hand off the steering wheel to hold up one finger. "And I'm not saying there is. But it could have more to do with my bank account than me."

"What makes you think that?" Damon asked. "The two of you were friends before, back when you were a working schmuck."

"Things have changed," Linc admitted. "I don't like change."

"Really? No one would have guessed when you have such an adventurous spirit. What did you have for breakfast today?"

"What does that have to do with anything?" Linc rolled to a stop at one of the few stoplights in Chatelaine and then turned toward the thrift shop.

"Just answer the question."

"I had a bowl of cereal."

"What did you have yesterday?"

"Also a bowl of cereal. Are you going to give me a lecture on adding protein to my morning diet? What's it to you, Damon?"

"You've been eating a bowl of cereal for breakfast since I can remember. You don't have to tell me or anyone that you don't like change. It's obvious from the way you live your life."

Linc felt a muscle tick in his jaw. "Can you blame me? When have I had the time for change or variety or trying new things? For years, I've been too busy with responsibilities, helping Mom, and trying to make sure my three doofus brothers stayed on the right path."

"We weren't your responsibility." Damon's tone changed from teasing to serious in an instant.

Linc couldn't remember his carefree youngest brother ever sounding so solemn.

He refrained from explaining that caring for his brothers and then Justine *had* been his responsibility. Their father had given it to him before he left for good.

Linc had never shared the details of that final conversation with anyone. He wasn't even sure his family knew it had taken place.

He'd told Remi a bit of it, but even she didn't know the details. Not yet. Although if there was anybody who would understand, she was that person.

"I know you aren't my responsibility anymore," he conceded. That was as much as he could offer. Old habits and all that.

They pulled into the thrift store parking lot. "I'm not sure what's going on with Remi, but I'm positive I don't need more responsibility in my life. We had a nice time in California. Can we leave it at that?"

"How nice?" Damon asked, brows wiggling, back to his usual self.

"I'm not sharing details, but I don't think I'm ready for more than a good time."

"You think that's what she wants?"

Linc shrugged. It wasn't as if he and Remi had

talked about the future or she'd made demands on him. He just assumed that spending the night together would change things, and he now saw that ignoring how much that terrified him had been the easy way out and not fair to Remi. She was his friend and deserved better. He wanted to give her that but didn't know if he could.

"If you all are only friends, maybe I'll ask her out. I still can't get over how she looked on New Year's Eve in that dress. Who knew Remi was hiding so much hotness under that GreatStore apron?"

Part of Linc's problem was he now knew every inch of what her purple apron covered. Even though he told himself that their night together in California had enabled him to scratch an itch and get it out of his system, the truth was way more complicated. He wanted more and didn't know how to handle that. For most of his life, he'd been focused on what he should do instead of what he wanted to do.

"So you're okay with that?" Damon prompted, and Linc realized he hadn't answered his brother. "You're okay with me taking Remi out?"

He pulled into the parking lot of the thrift shop and shut off the engine. "Stay away from Remi," he said.

Damon lifted a brow. "That's not fair if you aren't going to make a move. She's a great girl."

"She's always been great."

"But now I know she's also gorgeous. I can't see

her like I did before." He shrugged. "Maybe she's the one to make me want to settle down."

"Too bad you'll never know," Linc said. "Because this isn't up for debate. You won't be asking Remi out. Not now, and not ever." He knew he had no right to act possessive, but that didn't stop him.

Damon got out of the car and came around to the back to help Linc unload his donations. "Glad we cleared that up," he said with a knowing grin. "For the record, I respect you and what you're telling me, but not every guy will. Remi is a catch, and you better figure out whether or not you want to take a chance with her before it's too late."

Remi stared at Paul, trying to process the bomb he'd just dropped without appearing as shell-shocked as she felt.

"You can't shut down the book department," she said, happy that her voice didn't reveal the tumult of emotions swirling through her.

As she'd hoped, Paul had finally been promoted to permanent department manager. She knew they'd work well together and had been looking forward to sharing some new ideas she had for the book section. To realize one of his first duties was downsizing the book section felt like a punch to the gut.

He sighed and looked past her at the rows of brightly colored titles that she lovingly curated each month. "I'm sorry, Rem. It's not my decision. The mandate came down from corporate. GreatStore locations across the country are dismantling their designated book departments to expand the electronics sections. Technology is where it's at as far as profits."

"Books are important."

"People can read on their phones or tablets," Paul told her.

She knew he was trying to put a positive spin on something that broke her heart, but she couldn't understand how the company she felt so loyal to would eliminate the thing she loved most in the world. First, she'd lost Linc at GreatStore, and now her beloved books? It was simply too much.

"Any way people access books is good," Remi agreed, "but e-reading doesn't eliminate the value of physical books. The book department is special, Paul. Books are special. There isn't another store in Chatelaine that stocks close to the selection of titles we do."

"I get that." Paul looked both pained and irritated that she was pushing so hard. Remi wasn't exactly known for her fighting spirit, but this felt different. Managing the book department wasn't simply a job. Taking care of readers in her beloved town was essential to her identity.

"Nobody else has a children's section. Kids love coming in here to look at the books. What will they do without a children's book section?"

"Go to the library?" Paul offered weakly.

Remi loved the local library, but that wasn't the point. "Do you know how many parents have brought in their children over the years to pick out a book as a reward for a good report card or a special treat?"

Paul held up his hands. "Remi, this is not my decision. I'm sorry I can't change it. Maybe I can convince corporate to dedicate a couple of shelves in the back to children's books. We'll still stock a few bestsellers up by the registers. But…"

"What about me?" she asked as the pit in her stomach seemed to grow exponentially larger. She'd been so busy advocating for the books that she hadn't thought about what closing the department would mean for her. "Are you getting rid of me along with the books?"

"No, of course not. You're a valuable member of the staff. You'll be transferred to Electronics unless there's another department that interests you more. Maybe Housewares or Health and Beauty?"

"I don't want to sell lipstick," she muttered. "I want to sell books."

"That won't be an option starting in two weeks."

Her heart sank. "So soon?"

Paul nodded.

She wondered if the change would have happened if Linc had still been in charge. He valued books as much as she did. Well, maybe not quite as much but certainly more than Paul, whose idea of reading was scanning the back of a cereal box.

But Linc wasn't a part of her life at GreatStore any longer. She couldn't even be sure he wanted to be a part of her life outside the store.

Remi needed to stand on her own two feet. She should have learned by now that no one else would do it for her.

"Who knows about the change?"

"The folks at corporate, me and you. I made sure you were the first person I told so you'd have time to adjust. Corporate doesn't want to make a big deal of it."

"Because they know it's a lousy way to do business."

Paul's mouth thinned. "I don't know how to make this better."

"I know it isn't your fault," she said, then drew in a deep breath. "I'll find a way to get over it if I'm going to stay at GreatStore."

"Don't say that, Remi. It's bad enough we lost Linc. I'd hate for you to leave, too."

They'd lost Linc. Now she was losing her books. Could things get any worse?

"I'm not sure," she admitted, "but maybe it's time I think about my future differently. I appreciate you giving me a heads-up, and I agree that we should keep things under wraps for a while. I want to enjoy my final couple of weeks without having to answer questions or people feeling sorry for me."

"I promise it stays quiet. I'm truly sorry. But if I can speak as Paul your friend now..." He waited for her to nod. "Maybe something great will come of this. After all, it wasn't until Linc quit that the two of you started hanging out together outside of work. Some of us might even call it dating."

She felt her face flush. "I don't think Linc would

call it that," she said before thinking better of it. He'd been sweet this week when they'd had lunch together, but she'd made an excuse instead of accepting his dinner invitation. She needed to get her feelings under control first before she did something stupid and blurt out that she loved him.

"He's not the sharpest knife in the drawer when it comes to women, but it's clear he likes you."

"I appreciate the vote of confidence," she said with a sigh. "But I'm not sure it means much. Linc has the means to make any dream come true. I'm not exactly known for being exciting and adventurous. He could get almost any woman he wants, now that he's rich."

"You're nice and pretty," Paul said, and she appreciated his loyalty. "Plus, you liked Linc before he had money. That counts for something, Rem."

Sadly, Remi had the impression it was a mark against her as far as Linc was concerned. She'd never met a man so determined not to open his heart. She hadn't made any demands on him but had a feeling he was creating scenarios in his head that involved her shackling him with a ball and chain.

It wasn't fair, just like losing her book department wasn't fair. But both made Remi realize she'd been living her life for other people for far too long.

"Linc is a great guy no matter how many zeros are part of his bank account." She reached out and squeezed Paul's shoulder. "You're a good guy, too."

"Maybe I'll meet my own Remi Reynolds one day."

That made her laugh. "Oh, to be so lucky," she teased. Then she twirled like a celebrity on stage, although her heart still hurt at the thought of what her future would hold working in Electronics. She'd never minded going to work because she thought of the book department as her own little kingdom. Now she'd have to find another way to feel like she had a purpose.

"Hey, guys. What going on?"

As Linc approached from a nearby aisle, her heart seemed to skip a beat.

"Seriously, dude." Paul rolled his eyes. "You need to get a hobby."

"As a matter of fact." Linc held up a basket of merchandise. "I'm shopping for fishing gear because my new boat is being delivered on Friday."

Remi sucked in a breath, and Paul's eyes widened. "What kind of boat?"

"A twenty-three-foot Ranger with a three hundred horsepower outboard engine." Linc looked almost embarrassed as he shared the information, although it didn't mean much to Remi. "It's got all the bells and whistles you'd expect."

"That's awesome." Paul pumped his fist. "Top of the line. Nothing but the baller lake life for my high-roller friend."

"A little much." Linc smiled, winking at Remi.

She didn't return the grin. This wasn't a side of Linc she particularly enjoyed. Not that she begrudged him spending his money however he saw fit. It was his choice, after all. Like she'd told her new friend Martin at lunch, Linc was a good guy in his heart. Fancy cars and fast boats didn't make him more important or exciting, in her opinion.

"I'm picking it up over in Corpus Christi this weekend so thought I'd take it out for an inaugural spin on the lake." He frowned when she didn't react with obvious glee the way Paul did.

"Hey, Alec," Paul called, motioning over the third amigo in their trio. "Linc bought a boat. We're hitting the water this weekend."

"Killer," Alec said, giving Linc a hearty slap on the back. "We slay fish all day." He turned to Paul and tapped a finger on his watch. "You ready for the monthly meeting?"

Alec had been promoted at the same time as Paul and was now the assistant manager of the garden department at GreatStore.

Paul groaned. "I'll be sitting in a meeting, but I'll be dreaming of a cold beer on the boat's bow. See you later tonight, Linc."

"Our weekly basketball league," Linc explained to Remi as his two friends headed for the offices at the back of the store.

She nodded. "You don't owe me an explanation about your plans."

His brows drew together as he looked at her, his moss green eyes searching her face. "You and Paul seemed to be deep in conversation when I approached. Is everything okay?"

Not in the least, she wanted to answer, but nodded instead. "All fine here. I should go. We got in a new shipment yesterday. I want to make space for the books."

"I finished that mystery you recommended," he offered quickly before she could turn away. "You were right about it being a page-turner. Kept me up half the night." He swayed toward her. "Although it wasn't half as good as staying awake with you."

Her heart stuttered. How was she supposed to keep her distance when his flirtatious words made her want to fold herself into him?

"I'm glad you liked the book," she said, taking a step back instead of moving closer. "The other part, too."

He shifted the shopping basket to one hand and took a step toward her. She moved away again.

"Remi, what's wrong?" He looked genuinely confused—big dumb man. Could he not see that she was falling in love with him and trying to hold on to some shred of dignity? "Did something happen? You don't seem fine. You look upset."

There was no way for him to know about corporate's decision to remove the book section. No way for him to realize that she was having trouble keeping her heart safe when it flung itself against her ribs every time he was near.

"I have a lot of work," she lied. "Congratulations on your boat. I hope it makes you happy."

"You'll come out with us this weekend?"

She shook her head. "I don't really enjoy fishing."

"You told me your dad used to take you every weekend. Those were some of your favorite memories of him. I thought you'd love going boating with me."

Leave it to Lincoln to remember some obscure detail she'd shared. How was she supposed to answer? She'd love watching paint dry with Linc.

That was simply too embarrassing.

"You're right, but this weekend sounds more like a guys' trip. I'll come with you another time, maybe."

"Maybe?"

"I've got to grab those boxes of books." She reached out and patted his arm. "It was nice to see you today, Linc."

He blinked. "Have dinner with me tonight? I'm taking my mom to the LC Club again. She'd love for you to join us. I would, too."

"I have plans." She offered a smile that wobbled at the corners. "Another time. Say hi to your mom for me."

"Another time when?" he demanded, looking far less laid-back than usual. "Did I do something wrong, Remi? I know we haven't had much time together since California but—"

"I had such a good time on our trip," she told him. "But now I have to go."

Wimp, she inwardly chided, then turned on her heel and headed down the aisle toward the storeroom.

Chapter Twelve

"Are you sure you don't want to come with me?"

Remi glanced up from the sofa in her mother's living room, a heaping handful of popcorn nearly to her mouth. "I don't think I'd fit in too well with your Bunco group, Mom."

"Those ladies love you, Remi." Stella scowled as she watched Remi chew. "Microwave popcorn is not an appropriate dinner. Sharla is making a pot of black bean chili. At least you could get some good food, or I have leftover soup in the fridge. There are vegetables in it."

"Corn is a vegetable," Remi countered and licked a dribble of butter from her wrist. "I'm fine. There's a new season of *Housewives* to binge. I'm all good for tonight."

Her mother sniffed, clearly not fooled. "What happened to that eternal smile from a few days ago? Did you and Lincoln have a fight? Relationships can be fragile when they're new and—"

"Linc and I aren't in a relationship." Remi popped another piece of popcorn into her mouth. "We're friends."

"So you did have a fight?"

"No." Remi shook her head and scrolled up a few channels. "Linc is great. He bought a boat and invited me to go fishing this weekend."

"You love boating. I remember when you used to wake up before the sun rose to wait for your daddy in the kitchen."

"I'm not going," Remi said. "He's taking his friends."

"You're his friend."

"Yes, and he invited me and a bunch of other guys. I'll join them another time."

Her mother moved closer, her gaze infinitely gentle as she stared down at Remi. "What's going on? And don't tell me nothing. I know you better than that."

"I like him, Mom. Too much. I don't want to get hurt."

"Oh, sweet girl. You might think you're protecting yourself, but if you don't open your heart, nothing can fill it. You'll remain empty, and you deserve more than that."

"I just want to know it won't turn out badly in the end."

"There are no guarantees, but you can have adventures along the way. Take a chance. Don't let life pass you by without reaching for happiness. It's what your father would have wanted for you, Remi. I want it for you, too."

"I want adventure," Remi said with a sniff. "But I'm afraid. What if Linc doesn't want the same things I do? You and Dad had the perfect relationship. It's a lot to live up to."

"Hardly perfect," her mother said with a wistful smile. "But we never gave up or stopped trying. Sometimes you have to put everything on the line for the greatest payoff."

Remi thought about how unsure she felt with Linc now that their relationship was more than coworkers. Her unrequited crush had been simple in comparison. She blinked away tears and opened her mouth to tell her mother about the devastating news she'd received at work that day but shoved in another handful of popcorn instead.

"I'll think about that," she told her mother as she chewed, sounding more like "I f-wink bou dat."

"You dropped a piece on your sweatshirt." Stella shook her head. "If you change your mind about real food, text, and I'll bring home a doggie bag for you."

"Thanks, Mom. It makes me appreciate you and Dad even more to know it wasn't always easy."

Her mother smiled again as a car horn honked. "That's my ride. Call or text if you need anything. And remember, nothing worth having is easy."

Except for popcorn and reality television, Remi

thought as she settled into the new season of one of her favorite shows. She didn't usually indulge in self-pity, but tonight she needed an escape and watching other people whose lives were way more messed up than hers fit the bill.

Within minutes, she was bored to pieces and reaching for the book she'd placed on the coffee table. Her stomach also grumbled, and she thought about texting her mom. Sharla made the best chili.

When the doorbell rang, Remi jumped up from the sofa and dusted off popcorn crumbs as she bee-lined toward the front of the house. It would be a sign if her mother returned because she'd forgotten some-thing. A sign that Remi was due for some good food and laughs with her mom's close circle of friends.

She didn't stop to think about what it might say about her life that her best option for a girls' night out was Bunco with the hot-flash brigade.

"Did you forget your key?" she asked as she opened the door.

"I don't think I have one to your mother's house," Linc answered from where he stood on the other side.

For a heart-stopping moment, Linc wondered if Remi would slam the door in his face.

"I thought you were going to dinner with your mom," she said, looking past him like Kimberly might be standing in the front yard.

Linc was dedicated to his mom, but even he knew

better than to bring her along when he was trying to smooth things over with a woman.

"She ditched me," he explained, palms up. "She got a better offer. Some Bunco group needed a sub. To be honest, I don't even understand the point of Bunco."

Remi's lips twitched. "It's a dice game and an excuse to get together to eat, drink and gossip. My mom is part of that group. She invited me along tonight."

"But you're here?"

"I had other plans."

He took in her baggy sweatshirt and jeans with holes in both knees—fashionable holes but still. "Am I interrupting?"

She swiped the back of her hand across her mouth. "No. Honestly, I'm having popcorn for dinner and watching reality TV."

Linc didn't consider himself a guy with an over-inflated ego, but the idea of his dinner invitation being rebuffed for a night at home on the sofa took him down a peg or two. "Okay. Well, I stopped by to change your mind about going out with me tonight if you didn't have other plans. If you're busy…"

She tugged on her lower lip with her teeth and let out a big sigh. "I want to go to dinner with you."

"But…" he prompted.

"This feels odd." She gestured between the two of them. "I don't know what we are to each other since California. Our night together was…"

"Amazing," he supplied and offered a hopeful grin when she raised a brow.

"And also confusing, at least for me."

"I like you, Remi," he told her. "I hope you like me, too."

"You know I do."

"Then there's no cause for confusion. We don't have to complicate things by defining them." Linc knew he'd said the wrong thing when she narrowed her eyes.

Then her gaze cleared. "No complications. Got it. I think that helps me understand things better."

"Is that good?" he asked, wondering if he'd made some horrible mistake.

"For now." She nodded. "Come in while I get changed."

"I still have the reservation at the LC Club."

"We don't have to go someplace fancy."

"I'd like to take you out to a nice dinner."

He moved into the house's small entry and brushed a strand of hair away from her face. "I'd like to take you on a date, Remi."

"A date here in Chatelaine?" she asked like she didn't quite understand what he was telling her. "Because people will see us together. They'll guess that we're more than friends."

He traced his thumb along the shell of her ear. He knew from their one night together how sensitive her ears were. He wanted to discover what other parts were sensitive. He wanted to know everything about her, even if he wasn't ready to put labels on their relationship.

Labels and responsibilities had shackled Linc for too long. Right now, he wanted to enjoy Remi and their time together. He'd had plenty of time to think since their night together, and he was tired of playing it safe. Linc might not be ready to risk his heart, but he didn't want to let this moment pass. "I'm okay with people knowing about us." He searched her face. "Are you?"

Her expression cleared, and it gratified him to see the worry disappear from her lovely brown eyes.

"Yes." She rose up on tiptoe to kiss him. "It's more than okay. Give me five minutes, and I'll be ready."

He smiled as she took the steps two at a time.

"Help yourself to something to drink," she called from the second floor.

Instead of heading toward the kitchen, Linc moved into the cozy living room with the overstuffed plaid sofa and matching love seat. He grabbed a piece of popcorn out of the bowl on the coffee table.

He still didn't understand Remi's resistance earlier, but he was a mixed-up jumble of emotions most days and in no position to judge.

A fleece blanket had been draped over the sofa, and an open book sat on the armrest. As much as he wanted to treat Remi to a nice dinner with a view of Lake Chatelaine, he couldn't deny the appeal of this setup.

Linc had lived alone since moving from his mom's

house after high school. The first couple of years before he got promoted and made a decent salary at GreatStore had been hard, but he never wanted a roommate. Hell, he'd rarely invited any of the women he dated to his home.

After spending so many years with four siblings crammed into his mom's tiny house, he valued his privacy and space above almost anything else.

But he could imagine quiet nights cuddled up with Remi watching a show or with each of them reading. She'd chew her lip and twirl the ends of her hair, which he knew from seeing her for years in the GreatStore break room was her habit when she got really into a book.

The irony of not being able to define their relationship but imagining a future with her wasn't lost on him. He'd take it one day at a time.

One adventure at a time, and hopefully, that would be enough for them both. Linc had a feeling it was all he was able to offer, at least at this point.

He moved across the room to where several framed photographs sat on a display shelf. There was a photo of Remi at her high school graduation in her white cap and gown, flanked on either side by her mom and dad. Her grin spread from ear to ear, and her parents looked so proud.

What would it have been like to grow up the child of a happily married couple? He couldn't imagine, but it gave him a deeper understanding of why it was so easy for Remi to show affection.

She'd never had to hoard it or wonder if there was enough to go around.

Linc wished he knew how to feel that way.

"I'm ready."

His mouth dropped open as he turned and saw her. "You are beautiful," he said, trying not to gape. Remi wore a sweater dress in a deep forest green color. It gently hugged her curves and stopped just above her knees. She'd paired it with leather ankle boots, showing off her gorgeous legs. Her hair had been pulled back with wispy tendrils curling around her face. She looked amazing.

A hint of pink crept into Remi's cheeks, and she offered a shy smile. "I don't want to make you look bad now that you're part of the country club set."

Her words were teasing, but he heard a hint of uncertainty in her tone.

"Any man would be lucky to have you on his arm. It doesn't matter whether you're dolled up or going casual. You're a prize, Remi. Don't ever doubt it."

"Thank you," she said. "You're a prize, too, Linc. Not because you can now afford to hang with the rich and famous of Chatelaine. Remember, you have a lot more to offer people than your bank account."

He wanted to believe her, but what had he been able to give anybody before now? At least with money, he could take care of his family and friends. But this wasn't the time for self-doubt.

"Shall we go?" He held out his hand to her, and when her fingers touched his, it was like an electric current shot through him. Linking their fingers, he led her out the door, only to pause when she pulled up short.

"What's going—" He glanced around and realized what had caught her attention. Several of her mother's neighbors stood on the lawn next door, staring at his car.

"Hey, Mrs. Wyatt. Hey, there, Mr. Matthews," Remi called and waved with her free hand. She tried to tug her fingers out of Linc's, but he didn't release her.

"We heard about this fancy car," the older man said to Linc.

Remi's mother lived in one of the modest, established neighborhoods of Chatelaine. It was no surprise that the residents were interested in his Italian sports car.

"Maybe I'll let you take it for a spin one of these days," Linc answered.

The woman, Ada Wyatt, laughed. Linc recognized her immediately. She'd worked in the front office at the high school when he'd been a student. "You, too, Mrs. Wyatt," he added.

"That thing's too cramped for my big bones." She smacked her curvy hip. "But I bet our Remi would look good behind the wheel."

"Oh no," Remi protested without hesitation. "I'm content driving my base-model hatchback. Knowing my luck, I'd get behind the wheel of that thing and be pulled over for speeding."

"We should test that theory right now," Linc said, suddenly loving the idea of Remi driving his car. He hadn't let any of his brothers drive it, but he trusted her and wanted her to trust him—to trust that money hadn't changed him.

That seemed important to her, and he wanted to live up to those expectations.

He pulled the keys from his pocket and dropped them into her hand. "I think it's about time your luck changed."

There was a flash of something he didn't understand in her gaze. It looked like the saddest mix of hope and regret he'd ever seen. His instinct was to pull her close and comfort her for whatever problem weighed heavy on her mind.

But she blinked and smiled, waving the keys to the two older neighbors. "I warned him. You heard it."

"You're going to be great, Remi," the older man assured her, then chuckled. "It's just like driving a regular car, only it'll take half a year's salary to fix it if anything goes wrong."

She let out a little yelp. "That's not making me feel better."

"You'll be fine," Linc said.

She nodded and climbed into the driver's seat. "Lake Chatelaine, here we come." The engine purred to life, and she rolled down the window to give a thumbs-up to her neighbors.

Mrs. Wyatt held up her phone. "I'm going to document this for your mother. She'll love to see it."

Remi laughed, and whatever tension had been plaguing her earlier seemed forgotten. Linc liked making her feel lighter, almost as much as he liked how he felt when he was with her. Money might not be able to buy happiness, but it eased the path to it.

She put the car into gear and backed out of the driveway. The tires squealed as she hit the accelerator too hard and then slammed the brakes. His body jerked forward, the seat belt snapping over his chest.

"Are you sure this is a good idea?" she asked.

"Nice and slow. You've got this. It takes a steady hand."

"I've got this," she murmured, gripping the steering wheel with both hands. She shifted the car into Drive and headed out of the neighborhood.

She relaxed within a few blocks and asked him to turn on the radio, singing along to the popular dance tune that blared out of the sophisticated sound system.

Linc raised a brow when she took a right turn instead of a left toward the lake.

"I want to do a quick spin through downtown if you don't mind," she said with a shrug. "How else will people believe Remi Reynolds can handle an Italian sports car like I'm Mario Andretti."

"I don't mind. Whatever makes you happy."

"You make…" She coughed and cleared her

throat. "You make being filthy rich seem like a lot of fun."

He didn't think that was what she was about to say but didn't push her. Remi was respecting his boundaries, and he owed her the same consideration.

He placed a gentle hand on her arm. "Being with you is what makes it perfect."

Whatever issues she had with his willingness to define their relationship could be overcome. Linc would show her that he could make uncomplicated way more fun than the alternative.

Chapter Thirteen

Remi was on her knees sorting through the next month's magazines the following morning when Alana came bustling into the storeroom.

"Tell me everything," the bubbly blonde demanded. "Each tiny detail. I want to know it all. Also, do either of his brothers have their inheritance at this point? Not that I'm looking for a sugar daddy, but I wouldn't mind a little sweetness in my life at the moment."

"Everything about what?" Remi asked as she straightened.

"You were seen with a poop-eating grin on your face, driving through downtown in Lincoln Fortune Maloney's Ferrari."

"Right." Remi nodded. Why on earth had she thought it was a good idea to publicize her night out with Linc in such a blatant way?

She'd been car drunk. That was the only explanation because Remi typically hated attention. Based on her mixed-up feelings for Linc, the last thing she needed was an interrogation. Still...

"It was perfect," she admitted.

"Perfect isn't a detail." Alana retied her purple apron as she spoke.

"He let me drive the car, which was an adventure in and of itself. Did you know a Ferrari can go from zero to sixty in under five seconds?"

"Did not know. Do not care. I'm talking about the juicy bits. There's a rumor going around that you and Linc went somewhere together on a private plane. I have a feeling Alec and Paul know the details. I know his brothers do. I can't get anybody to tell me, but you outdid yourself with this parade through downtown."

"We drove through on a weeknight. That's hardly a parade."

"You know what it means around here. So you must have wanted to be seen."

"We were going on a date to the LC Club. I figured we'd be outed anyway. So I did want to be seen with Linc."

"And that hot car," Alana added.

"The car is fun, but I don't care about it. I care about Linc. I'm not the kind of woman anybody would expect him to date. Maybe it's petty that I wanted people to see me with him, but—"

"Why wouldn't he want to date you?" Alana

screwed up her face into a pucker like she was trying to puzzle out Remi's claims.

If Remi made that face, she'd look ridiculous. Even with a funny-looking expression, Alana was adorable.

"You know what I mean," Remi insisted.

"I know Linc doesn't do serious relationships. If that's what you're looking for, it could be an issue. Or perhaps money has changed his perspective on things."

"It's not the money or his perspective on relationships." Remi yanked on the ponytail she wore almost every day to work. "It's because I'm not his type. He dates women who are gorgeous and vivacious and fun. Women like you, Alana. He didn't even recognize me at first on New Year's Eve."

Alana shook her head. "He certainly seemed to like knowing it was you once he realized it. I know hair, makeup and whatever are not your thing, but it doesn't have to be about that. There are a lot of other reasons Linc would want to date you. Any man would."

"Funny," Remi said without laughing. "That's exactly what Linc said."

"Was he volunteering to be that guy?" Alana asked.

"He acts like he wants to, but he also doesn't want to define things."

Her friend seemed to think about that as she lowered herself onto one of the nearby chairs.

"How does that make you feel?"

"Fine," Remi said, then shook her head. "No. It

makes me feel like I'm not enough. Maybe if I had something more to offer, he would want more."

"What more could the guy want? It sounds like he's got enough money to pick anyone, and he hasn't exactly been shy about spending it. The fact that you and Linc are growing closer even with his change of circumstances means something—something good."

"I guess I need to give him a little time."

"Right," Alana agreed. "The guy's had a lot of changes in his life, and he isn't the sort of man who seems to thrive on change."

"We have that in common," Remi said with a laugh.

"You have a lot in common."

"Thanks, Alana. You're different than a lot of people think. I appreciate you listening to me. I know you're right. Plus, I'm not completely sure that I'm going to be staying in Chatelaine much longer."

The other woman's bright eyes widened. "What are you talking about?"

"Can you keep a secret?"

"With my life."

"They're eliminating the book section here at GreatStore."

"No. Why?"

"I guess it isn't doing as well as it needs to. They're expanding Electronics. Paul told me last week, but I made him promise to keep the information quiet a little longer."

"Are you transferring to another department? You wouldn't leave GreatStore. Wait, is that your plan?"

Remi shrugged. "I don't exactly have a plan yet, but I applied for a job at a bookstore in San Antonio."

"Seriously? You'd leave Chatelaine? What about your mom? I know how close the two of you are."

Remi bit down on her lower lip. "We are, but I came home to help her after my dad died. I never planned to stay here permanently."

"This is your home."

"I'm going to take some time to think about it, and my relationship with Linc is part of that. No matter what happens with him, I want my life to have a purpose. I don't know if selling electronics will do that for me. If the only reason I'm staying here is that I'm afraid of change, that's not a very good reason, is it?"

"I guess not," Alana agreed. "You should do what makes you happy, but I hope you find a reason to stay. I know we're not close, but lately, the importance of surrounding myself with good people has...well, it's important, and you're one of the best people I know."

"You're pretty great as well," Remi said and reached out to hug the coworker who suddenly felt like a friend.

"Is this a private hug, or can anyone get in on it?"

Remi pulled away and smiled as Alec approached.

"Way to ruin a tender moment," Alana said.

"Ruining moments is my specialty," their friend declared, making both women laugh.

"Speaking of ruining moments..." Alec leveled a stare at Remi. "I'm here to convince you to join us on Linc's boat tomorrow. He's threatening to sell the thing before taking it out for an inaugural day on the water. Paul and I think you could convince him that Captain Maloney is a good look on him."

Remi shrugged. "What Linc does with his money isn't my business. I'm sure he can decide on his own."

Alana nudged her. "Maybe he needs another reminder about why certain decisions might be better than others."

"Yeah, like the decision to keep an awesome boat," Alec agreed. "Come on, Remi."

"I'll go if Alana does."

Alana clapped her hands. "You don't have to ask me twice. I happen to be off tomorrow, and it's supposed to be an unseasonably warm day. Boating sounds like a perfect way to spend it."

Alec grinned and gave each of them a thumbs-up. "We've got our boat babes. I love it."

"You're not allowed to call us boat babes," Alana told him.

"Got it." Alec nodded. "How about boat bi—"

"Stop right now," Remi said with a laugh. "Before you dig yourself in any deeper."

"Understood. I'll tell Linc the boating adventure is on."

Remi turned and offered Alana a high five. "Here's to more adventures."

Linc thanked the manager at the laser tag center in Corpus Christi and headed toward the party room where his friends were engaged in various arcade games.

He noticed Remi standing at the edge of the hallway, staring at her phone with what looked like a mix of shock and excitement. He wondered who she was messaging, and a vision of that guy she'd gone on a date with weeks ago formed an unwelcome picture in Linc's brain. It couldn't be him. She hadn't even liked him.

Linc didn't understand why he suddenly felt so unsure about the status of his relationship with a woman who'd been his friend for years. After all, he was the one who'd made it clear he couldn't commit to anything serious and didn't want to define what was going on between them.

Part of him didn't like how easily she'd accepted his reluctance for any sort of commitment.

"Is everything okay?" he asked as he got closer to her.

She looked up and quickly shoved her phone into the back pocket of the slim jeans she wore. "All good. I was confirming an appointment I have next week."

He had no reason not to believe her. It was none of his business if she didn't want to share details.

"I'm sorry about the boat. The manufacturer promised me it would arrive by today, and I paid extra to confirm it. The good news is the manager here told me he'd be willing to close early to the general public so we can have it all to ourselves."

"Linc, we don't need it all to ourselves."

"Well, I want to make it feel special since I let everybody down on the plan for today."

Remi put a hand on his arm. "Issues happen. It's not your responsibility to provide amazing experiences or gifts or financial support for your friends and family."

"But I can," he countered. "What else am I going to do with the money? I want to make sure the people I care about have fun. You were the one who talked to me about experiences being more important than materialistic stuff. Why the sudden change of heart?"

She gave him a funny look. "My heart hasn't changed."

The sincerity in her voice caused his chest to tighten, not painfully but more as a reminder of how much his heart reacted to this woman.

"I know you can give the people around you the time of their life, but even that…" She shrugged and searched his face. "Does it fulfill you?"

He made a show of glancing around the fun center because he was afraid of what might be revealed if he met her gaze. "I don't know that anyone would describe laser tag as fulfilling, but I'm having fun. Is that so wrong?"

"Fun," she repeated like she was testing how the word tasted on her tongue. "Fun is good. Just remember that it doesn't take money to have fun."

"Tell that to Alec and Paul and my brothers." He tugged a hand through his hair. "Why are you the person I want to spoil, and you're the only one who seems not to care about my money?"

"Because you're more important than your bank account, Linc. One of these days I'm going to make you understand that." She suddenly looked inspired. "In fact, let's start tonight. Do you have dinner plans?"

He shook his head and then sighed. "No, but I figured the guys would want me to take everyone out."

"No. You and I are going to have a night together. A fun night. Just the two of us."

"I like the sound of that," he said, leaning closer. He hated to admit he was beginning to feel desperate to be with Remi again. Their date at the LC Club had ended with a few heated kisses in the Ferrari. She'd insisted she couldn't do the drive of shame home from his house in the wee hours when half the town was probably already talking about the two of them being together.

She placed her hands on his biceps and squeezed.

"What time should I pick you up?" he asked.

"I'll come to you."

"It's a good thing my luxury bed sheets arrived last week."

She threw back her head and laughed. "Lincoln Fortune Maloney, if you think we need expensive sheets to make it a good night, you haven't been paying attention."

"Right," he agreed. "What sort of food should I order?"

"I'll take care of everything," she told him. "You just be prepared for a great evening."

He opened his mouth to argue. Even before his inheritance, Linc wasn't used to giving up control.

Had he ever let a girlfriend plan a date?

Was Remi his girlfriend?

He'd said no labels, but the idea of having her as his girlfriend officially felt like a puzzle piece finding the exact place it fit.

"I'll do my best," he said and pressed a quick kiss to her mouth. She tasted like cinnamon gum. "But first, I'm going to kick your butt at Skee-Ball."

"We'll see about that," she said and led him toward the arcade.

Chapter Fourteen

Linc had just finished shoving the last of the week's internet shopping deliveries into his spare bedroom when the doorbell rang. He understood Remi's point about money not buying happiness. The first thing she saw when she walked in would not be the evidence that he was living under the opposite principle at the moment.

Seriously, though. That electric weed whacker he'd seen on the TV would come in handy once he got around to upgrading the landscaping in his yard. It only made sense that he bought one for himself as well as each of his brothers.

He opened the door to a smiling Remi holding a giant shopping bag in one hand and a bike helmet in the other. Her hair was pulled back into a low ponytail, and she wore a backpack so overstuffed it looked like she might topple over, turtle-style, from its weight.

"Did you ride your bike here?"

She nodded and offered a shy smile. "I told my mom I wouldn't be home until tomorrow morning and thought it would be better if my car weren't here overnight. You understand, right?"

Before he could answer, she continued, "I put my bike to one side of your garage, so it's not obvious to your neighbors." She grimaced as she gestured to the piles of empty boxes currently occupying his front porch. "Although maybe no one would have noticed."

He took the bag and helmet from her as he stepped into his house. "Remi, I don't care if people know you're staying here. I'm not embarrassed or—"

She placed a finger against his lips. "I'm not embarrassed, either. But we've agreed not to put labels on our relationship. It's a small town, Linc. I get that people already know or have guessed that we're more than friends. I still don't want to advertise it out of respect for myself and my mom."

He thought about that as she took off her backpack. "Am I disrespecting you? Because that's the last thing I want. I like you, Rem. You're one of the best people I know."

Her smile was both sad and sweet, a combination he didn't like associating with himself as the cause.

"Not to be all cliché," she told him, "but this is about me, not you. Keeping things casual and loose doesn't exactly come naturally to me, but I'm trying.

At the same time, I'd rather not be a topic of conversation around the GreatStore break room, if you know what I mean?"

"I do." Linc nodded and forced himself to smile. Remi was different than other women he'd dated. Even when he'd insisted on keeping things casual in the past, the women he'd been with had seemed interested in doing everything they could to either change his mind or make their association so public that he wouldn't have a choice but to commit.

Linc had learned a powerful lesson about commitment from his father. There was always a choice. And if he was forced into a relationship, what would stop him from hurting somebody the way his father had broken his mother?

That was the last thing Linc would ever want, primarily where Remi was concerned. He should probably thank her for insisting they keep their association private.

So why did he have the urge to shout it from the rooftops?

"What do we have on the agenda tonight?"

"You're going to love this." She grinned and unzipped her backpack, handing him a plastic container of…he couldn't quite tell. It looked like a white blob.

"We're making homemade pizza and playing board games," she announced with a smile. "I made the dough earlier so all we have to do now is roll it out and add the toppings."

Of all the ways Linc could have imagined spending an evening, making dinner and playing board games had never crossed his mind.

Remi's smile wavered as he continued to stare at the dough blob.

"I know it's probably boring compared to how you're used to spending your evenings now that you can afford any adventure money can buy, but give it a chance. Can you do that?"

He shook his head and then quickly nodded. "It doesn't seem boring."

"Pathetic?" she suggested with a self-conscious laugh.

He thought about recent nights spent trying to fill the endless hours he had without work or other commitments. Mindlessly scrolling the internet, channel surfing, or compulsively buying stuff he didn't need. He'd managed to subscribe to every cable service offered and still, most evenings, couldn't find anything to hold his attention. The irony of surrounding himself with so much and still being bored out of his mind wasn't lost on Linc. It felt easier to fill his house than his life, just as Remi had told him.

"It sounds perfect." He took the backpack from her and peered inside. "I sure hope you brought pepperoni."

"Along with three different kinds of cheese."

He followed her into the kitchen, where she placed the topping selections in bowls and pulled gadgets out of the drawers like she belonged there.

It felt as though she belonged there.

She filled him in on the latest gossip and customer stories from GreatStore, and he laughed and offered his opinion on a few of the stickier staff situations. Of course she'd also been right about him needing a purpose.

He missed having a reason to get out of bed and start his day every morning. The hours might have been long and the job stressful, but he'd been contributing something to the world.

As much as he gave it his best try, Linc wasn't sure he was cut out to be a man of leisure and simply taking a couple of classes felt almost indulgent compared to his previous work schedule.

He started to apologize for his ancient oven as the door squeaked and then stuck when she went to open it. The appliance was a relic from the last renovation of the house, circa mid-seventies, by his estimation.

"New appliances," he said, holding up a hand. "That's my next mission. Maybe I'll get the whole kitchen redone. Do you know they make refrigerators that dispense fizzy water?"

"Is that so?" she asked, not appearing the least bit concerned about the age of his appliances. She put in the tray of pizza and closed the oven door. At least the thing still got hot.

"You like fizzy water," he reminded her as if she'd forgotten.

"Linc, if you want to buy new appliances, that's great. But it isn't the point of being in the kitchen together."

"I could buy a whole new house," he said. "I could

build a house. That's what Coop wants to do with his money."

"Do you want a new house for new appliances?"

He shrugged. "To be honest, I haven't turned on the stove in... I can't remember how long it's been."

"You sprinkle cheese like an expert," she told him. She wiped her hands on a dish towel and then drew closer, her expression gentle. "If you want a new house or a new kitchen or whatever, that's fine. You don't have to worry about what you can buy or where you can go."

She placed her soft hands on either side of his face. The touch both soothed and aroused him. "Let's be here right now and not think about what the future might hold."

He couldn't help feeling like there was a message he was missing in her words. But he liked the idea of letting everything go to concentrate on the moment. He kissed her long and slow, hoping to communicate without the words that seemed to fail him exactly how important she'd become in his life.

The words would come if they were meant to. He and Remi had all the time in the world. There was no reason to feel any pressure.

She melted against him for several minutes, then pulled back as the smell of melting cheese and roasted garlic filled his small kitchen.

Yeah, he could renovate or buy something new. Right now, it didn't matter. What was important was the two of them, here together.

They ate dinner at his small kitchen table and then moved to the sofa in the family room, where she kicked his butt at Scrabble and Clue.

"I demand a rematch," he said. "I don't think this is an equitable setup. You have an advantage."

She laughed. "What kind of advantage?"

"You keep distracting me by leaning forward."

She looked down at her simple V-neck sweater as if seeing it for the first time. Then her grin turned mischievous. "I'm distracting you. Is that the problem?"

She tugged on the sleeve and revealed the lacy strap of a bright pink bra. "Is this a distraction?"

His mouth went suddenly dry, but he managed to nod. "The best kind."

"Then I have one more game we should play."

He nodded enthusiastically. "I'm in."

"I haven't even told you what it is."

"Doesn't matter if it involves more distractions. I'll play it all night long."

"Strip Scrabble," she said, and he blinked.

"Is that a thing?"

"It can be."

"I'm going to win."

"You haven't won a single game we've played."

"I was lacking motivation."

He reached out a hand and traced one finger along her delicate collarbone. "Or we can skip the Scrabble part and go straight to the stripping."

He felt her breath grow shallow and saw a hint of pink color her neck. Finally, she nodded. "As much as I wanted to prove we could have as much fun on a night that didn't involve spending extra money or doing something out of the ordinary, I have to admit…" She bit down on her lower lip. "I'm intrigued by those sheets you mentioned."

"You want me for my sheets?"

"I want you, full stop," she countered.

Linc groaned as he took her arms and drew her closer, lifting her until she straddled his legs.

He hadn't realized how much the uncertainty over where they stood in their relationship had been weighing on him. So many things were changing in his life, complications he hadn't foreseen back in the summer when Martin Smith had given him the check.

He needed something—someone—steady, and Remi was exactly that. She'd been a loyal friend. Although his feelings were growing into something more, she remained a part of his life he knew he could depend on.

No amount of money could offer the measure of happiness he felt at this moment.

And he would do his damnedest to show her how much he appreciated her.

He deepened the kiss, their tongues swirling together in an intimate dance. When it felt like he would go crazy from just her mouth against his, he broke off and trailed kisses along her jaw. At the same time, he took hold of the hem of her sweater and lifted it up and over her head.

Her skin was almost as pink as the lacy bra, and

he lowered his head to lick a trail along her sweet skin. He pushed down the straps until her breasts were revealed to him, then covered one puckered tip with his mouth.

She said his name on a sigh and shifted against him, eliciting a groan from deep in his throat.

"It's all fun and games until somebody loses an *I*," he said, blowing cool air against her skin before sucking gently.

She bit off a choked laugh and wiggled, her clever hand working at the buttons of his jeans.

When her fingers dipped under his boxer's waistband, he wrapped his arms around her hips and lifted her as he rose from the sofa.

She sucked gently on the sensitive place under his jaw, and he practically lost his footing, kicking the coffee table as he righted them both. Game pieces went flying, and Remi laughed even harder.

"I win," she whispered into his ear as he beat an urgent path toward his bedroom.

"We both win," he countered, intending to prove it to her all night long.

Remi wasn't sure whether to be excited or terrified as she drove home from San Antonio three days later. The bookstore interview had gone better than she could have hoped. The assistant manager, whose position was coming open, was going back to school for a master's degree in the spring, but they wanted her replacement to begin in mid-February to have time to get up to speed.

To Remi's shock, they'd offered her the job at the end of the interview. The bookstore was in a bustling neighborhood south of downtown, and she could picture herself living there.

She was excited about the possibility and already had ideas for how she might take the somewhat tired space and transform it into something more vibrant.

As much as it was a great opportunity in theory, the truth in her heart was that she didn't want to leave her hometown or her friends and her mom.

She definitely didn't want to leave Linc now that things seemed to be progressing.

Their quiet night together had changed and strengthened their connection. They still didn't talk about defining their relationship, but he certainly acted like her boyfriend. Instead of showing up at GreatStore to buy unnecessary items, Linc made no secret that he stopped by to see her.

What would happen if she moved away? She didn't want to decide her future solely based on a man, but there was no denying that Linc was a factor.

It was hard to know how he'd react when she hadn't even told him about the book section going away.

As promised, Paul had kept the news under wraps, and Alana hadn't shared it, either. Of course, Remi had discussed the situation with her mother. It was clear Stella wanted her daughter to stay in Chatelaine but would support Remi in whatever she chose.

So why hadn't she told Linc? He'd always been important to her, but now she could say without a doubt she was in love with him. Not just a schoolgirl-crush kind of love. She wanted to build a life together.

There was no building a strong foundation without honesty, but fear held her back. She knew he was still uncertain about his own future despite the freedom Wendell Fortune's inheritance offered. She didn't want to put any pressure on him or make him feel like he owed her or was responsible for her happiness somehow.

She was in charge of her destiny—or liked to believe that was true. She'd read someplace that courage was doing the right thing even when afraid.

Remi certainly wasn't feeling courageous at the moment.

Like a sign from the universe, she heard a loud pop, and then her car began to shutter and thump as she drove the two-lane highway that led toward Chatelaine. A flat.

She pulled to the side of the road and got out of the car, confirming her suspicion. Her rear passenger-side tire had a giant chunk out of it. Maybe this was a test for her when it came to handling her own business.

Her father had taught her how to change a flat tire when she'd gotten her driver's license in high school, although she'd never had the need to try her skills in real life.

She glanced down at the trim pants and silk blouse

with a matching jacket she'd worn for the interview. At least the pants were black, and she kept an extra sweatshirt in the cargo hold of her car. She quickly took off the blazer, donned the sweatshirt, and then hauled the spare tire from its compartment.

She went over the steps in her head, positioning the jack under the car and then cranking it. Her dad would have been proud of her, and she had to admit she felt strong and independent. The whole back of her car lifted off the ground, and she'd done that without anyone's help.

Unfortunately, that was where things stopped progressing. No matter how hard she tried, Remi could not get the final lug nut to loosen.

Several cars sped by, but no one stopped, which was fine. Remi wanted to handle this on her own. She needed to pass this test.

A few more minutes of struggle elapsed with no progress. Glancing at her watch, she straightened and kicked the flat for good measure.

The nut refused to give. She was about fifteen minutes outside of town, so calling her mom or the local mechanic they'd used for years wouldn't be a huge deal.

Linc was an option as well, although she felt strangely uncomfortable with the idea of asking him for help.

She grabbed her cell phone from the front seat and was about to dial when a familiar truck pulled up behind her car.

"Linc," she breathed.

"You okay?" he asked as he strode toward her, mirrored sunglasses covering his eyes.

"Just a flat." She glanced up and down both sides of the empty highway. "What are you doing out here?"

"Hank Moore called. Said he'd passed your car but was late for a doctor's appointment so hadn't been able to stop. He thought I'd want to know."

"Thanks for coming," she said, tugging on the hem of the sweatshirt.

"Why didn't you call me, Remi?" He drew closer and bent to retrieve the lug wrench.

"I didn't want to bother you." Her throat felt tight as her uncertainty about their status warred with her feelings for him. "And I wanted to handle it on my own. There's one stupid nut that's stuck. I'm not strong enough."

"You're plenty strong. It's okay to need help."

"My dad taught me how to change a tire," she explained. "I wanted to prove that I could do it but didn't anticipate it being so hard." She glanced at the dusty ground when her voice cracked.

"Look at how far you've gotten," Linc said gently.

"But I couldn't finish," she insisted. Another car drove by, probably someone else who'd recognize her and realized that Remi Reynolds had needed a man to rescue her. "I don't know why I'm making it mean something, but it does. I can't stop it."

"Then let's finish together. Trust me, Remi." He squeezed her shoulders. "I'm an expert at wanting to manage life on my own. It doesn't always work that way. You're the person who's helped me see that."

"I have?" She sniffed and knelt next to him, not caring about dust or dirt on her pants. She might not want to need help but couldn't deny that she appreciated Linc being here for her.

"You would have managed it on your own eventually," she told him. "I have faith in you."

He smiled at her and then attached the wrench to the stubborn lug nut. "The point is that neither of us has to."

She drew in a breath as he put pressure on the nut. Was it any wonder she'd fallen head over heels for Linc when he said things like that? Remi wasn't a flowers and jewelry type of woman. She liked meaning and sincerity.

She liked the thought of not being alone, but even more she liked the idea of Linc as the person she could call on.

It took him a few tries, but he got the nut unstuck and then sat back on his heels. "Let's see how you do with the rest of it."

She stifled a giggle and shook her head. "You've come this far. I think you can handle it."

"It's funny," he told her, "because I know you can handle it as well."

It was the kind of thing her father would have said to her. Her dad had been a man's man. He'd liked hunting and fishing and watching football every weekend during the fall season.

About a year after he died, she'd asked her mom if he'd ever been disappointed that he only had girls, particularly one who was more interested in reading than sports, even if she liked fishing.

Stella had looked at Remi like she'd grown two heads and explained that her father had only ever been grateful for his daughters.

She was just as grateful for him.

She felt self-conscious with Linc watching but continued to follow the steps her dad had taught her to replace the flat.

Link made noises of approval, high-fived her when she finished, and then lifted the old tire into the back of her small car.

"That was impressive," he said, closing the hatch. "And weirdly sexy."

She grinned and wiped her hands on a napkin she found in the glove compartment. "It feels like an accomplishment. First, we tried strip Scrabble. Now car maintenance. Who knows what other aphrodisiacs we can discover together?" She walked to the back of her car and kissed him. "Thank you again for coming. I was about to call my mom or the auto shop when you showed up."

"You can always call me," Linc said, nuzzling her ear. "That's what friends are for."

His words were like a bucket of ice water dumped over her head. Right. She was madly in love with him, and he considered her a friend with strip-Scrabble benefits.

Maybe today had been a message from the universe after all, just not the kind she'd wanted or expected. A necessary reminder all the same.

"What are you doing out here, anyway?" Linc asked, finally noticing her outfit with the wedge heels and tailored pants on the bottom paired with a Cowboys sweatshirt on top.

She should tell him the truth. Given what he thought about the status of their relationship, it probably wouldn't bother him to think of her leaving Chatelaine. Maybe it would come as a relief. They could continue being friends with naked perks, just from a distance.

But it bothered Remi, both to think of her relationship with Linc being defined so narrowly and to seriously admit she was considering leaving her hometown.

"I met a friend for lunch," she said, hating herself for lying but unwilling to tell him the truth quite yet. "I thought I'd use driving to the city as an excuse to get dressed up. That didn't work out as well as I'd hoped."

"I like the sweatshirt and heels combination." He kissed her again. "You're beautiful no matter what."

She appreciated the words, although they also made her heart ache. She knew that wasn't his intention, but she loved him. Her heart wanted her to take a risk.

If only hearts were as easy to fix as a flat tire.

Chapter Fifteen

Friday afternoon, Linc parked across the street from the Hotel Fortune in the bustling town of Rambling Rose, which felt like a small-town metropolis compared to the quiet streets of Chatelaine.

He'd felt the same sense of awe when he'd made the drive to attend his sister's wedding the previous summer.

Before that, Linc hadn't been to Rambling Rose since he was a kid. Back then, the town had seemed similar to his own. Now this town had eclipsed Chatelaine in almost every way.

It was hard to believe that one family, the Fortunes, had produced so much change in the former cow town. He had even more difficulty associating himself with that family name.

But the challenge of being a man with the power

that money could generate was why he was there today. He also wanted to see his sister. Justine's relationship with the family had taken a hit because of their mother's initial reaction to her pregnancy. But Linc could have done a better job of making sure he and his brothers stayed close to their baby sister.

As the youngest, she would be the last to receive her inheritance. Ironically, Justine was also the most settled—and possibly mature—of his siblings.

Although the relationship had started with some complications, her marriage to Stefan Mendoza appeared to be a true love match.

He'd thought that perhaps after things got better with their mom that Justine might return to Chatelaine with her new family, but she seemed content in Rambling Rose.

He couldn't blame her for loving this town, with its eclectic Western vibe and vibrant energy. Linc wasn't interested in becoming a real estate developer but eyeing the busy streets of Rambling Rose made him wonder if there was some way he could use his wealth to benefit his local community.

Maybe Justine would have some ideas for him. He crossed the street and entered the hotel, whose rich wood trim and decor took inspiration from the art and architecture of the West.

Justine immediately waved from across the lobby and ended her conversation with a petite blonde.

"Hey, big brother," she said with a wide smile,

opening her arms for a hug. "To what do I owe the pleasure of this visit?"

"Can't a guy take his baby sister to lunch?"

She chucked him on the arm. "Be honest. Were you just looking for an excuse to take that fancy Ferrari on a road trip?"

"How did you know about…" He rolled his eyes. "Mom."

"She's worried about you getting a speeding ticket. Did you know red cars get pulled over more than vehicles of other colors?"

"I did because she's told me about a dozen times. It's a myth, and I don't speed."

Justine faked a cough.

"Much," he amended. "Do you want to take a ride?"

"Later." She gestured to the restaurant off the lobby. "Let's get lunch first."

"Is Stefan going to be able to join us?"

"Maybe," she answered, leading Linc toward a table near a high window. "He's swamped at work. The beer business is doing well."

"This place also seems to do a heck of business. I thought things were busy when we were down here last summer for your wedding. The town's popularity doesn't seem to be waning in the least."

"Rambling Rose is a wonderful place." She eyed him. "And home to plenty of Fortunes, old and new. Are you thinking of spreading your wings now that you have no responsibilities or reason to stay in Chatelaine?"

Linc squared his shoulders and glanced at the menu the hostess had given him. He knew his sister didn't have the same feelings about their hometown as he did, especially once things had gotten complicated with Kimberly.

"I have reasons to stay in Chatelaine." An image of Remi popped into his mind, but he quickly pushed it aside. He could not—would not—become too committed to their relationship. That was a surefire way to let her down. It was what was in his blood.

"But what is there to do now that you aren't working at GreatStore?" she asked as the waiter poured water and then took their drink orders.

Linc and Justine both asked for unsweetened iced tea, but he wished he could switch to a Long Island iced tea instead. He hadn't expected his little sister to grill him on his future.

"I'm finding ways to keep myself out of trouble," he said with a forced laugh, turning his attention to the menu. "What do you recommend?"

"Everything is good. I know it sounds basic, but you won't be disappointed if you like a club sandwich."

"A club sandwich it is," Linc told the waiter when he returned. He added sweet potato fries, which he promised to share with Justine since she ordered a salad.

"I came down to talk about you, not me," he said. "How are you, sis? Do you need anything? I've got this big bank account now and—"

"I'm living the dream," she answered with a bright

smile. "This time last year, I couldn't have imagined how good things would become. Life has exceeded all my expectations."

"Marriage clearly agrees with you."

"Speaking of marriage." She rolled her eyes when he made a show of choking and thumping his chest. "Be serious, Linc. Mom told me you're seeing someone. Not one of your typical casual flings."

"Wow, you and Mom are burning up the phone lines. I take it things are going well with the two of you?"

"We're working on it. Morgan has made forgiveness easier for me. Mom dotes on him, and I want my son to have a strong bond with his meemaw."

"She wants that, too."

"I know." Justine nodded, flipping her long blond hair over one shoulder. She wore a flowing, flower-patterned dress, which reminded Linc of the girly dresses and princess outfits she'd favored as a child. "We'll get there." She pointed a finger in his direction. "Now, stop changing the subject. We're talking about you."

"There's not much to talk about."

"A girlfriend?"

"We're not putting labels on it."

Justine groaned. "Spoken like the commitment-phobic big brother I know and love."

"I'm not averse to commitment." He paused to take a long drink of tea as the waiter brought their meals. For some reason, this conversation with Justine made Linc break out in a cold sweat. "You know I'm responsible. Dad leaving the way he did gave me no choice."

Justine paused with her fork in midair. She inclined her head to study him, and he resisted the urge to squirm. "I'm talking about falling in love and building a life with someone, Linc. It's not supposed to feel like a chore or a weight around your neck. When things are right, you feel lighter, not heavier."

He picked up a fry and then placed it on the plate again, his stomach churning too much to think about eating. "I'm not built for falling in love," he said quietly.

"Everyone has the capacity to fall in love," she said. "You just need to be willing to risk everything for it."

Linc knew his sister's life hadn't been easy. She'd never even known their father. In some ways, that was a blessing as far as Linc was concerned. At least Justine didn't have to deal with feeling like she'd done something wrong to make her father leave.

"Maybe," he conceded. "But falling in love and standing strong when things aren't easy are two different things. Rick couldn't handle the latter, so—"

"You're not him."

"I guess." Linc was afraid he was enough like his father that he could make the same mistakes and hurtful choices Rick had made back in the day.

Those choices had caused their mom a lifetime of pain and left each of Rick's children with invisible scars. His sister spoke of risk, but Linc wouldn't risk hurting someone he cared about in that same way.

Thankfully, Justine changed the subject to less complicated topics. She told him about the latest updates in Rambling Rose and scrolled through a dozen or so photos of little Morgan on her phone.

"Is that Martin Smith?" Linc asked as he studied a picture of Morgan on a swing at the playground with an older man standing behind him.

Justine nodded. "Morgan loves Martin." She said it like it was a fact. "We don't see him often, but he's so sweet with Morgan."

"Does he talk about the next installment of the inheritance?" Linc asked. "It's odd that he dumped a whole bunch of zeros on me and then took off. I think Max is getting worried his check is lost in the mail."

"I'm sure Martin has a master plan. He doesn't talk about it a lot, but I get the impression he's happy to be able to share Wendell's fortune with us. It gives him some purpose."

Purpose. It seemed everyone was obsessed with having a purpose. "Do you think about Wendell Fortune being our grandfather? In Rambling Rose, especially, it seems like the Fortune name goes a long way. Is it better to feel like a Fortune than a plain old Maloney?" He dipped a fry into the ramekin of ketchup the waiter had brought. "Although, I guess you can claim a new identity as a Mendoza now."

"I consider myself all of those," Justine told him. "Mostly I think about trying to be the best version of myself." She sounded much wiser than her twenty-five years as she spoke.

"More than anything else, I consider myself a mom and try to live in a way that honors the world and the future I want for my son. Yes, being a Mendoza is a big part of that. Of course, our childhood also shaped me into the person I am. It shaped all of us, for better or worse. As far as being a Fortune... Let's just say the Fortune name has many connotations for many people. But ultimately the Fortunes are people, just like the rest of us."

"Wealthy people," Linc clarified.

"Some of them." Justine shrugged. "Most of them, maybe. But wealthy people have problems and struggles, too. Different from the ones we faced growing up, but no less influential for them. Obviously, Wendell Fortune struggled. Even if Dad had known about his father, I don't think it would have changed who he was. Maybe if he'd had a relationship with Wendell, it would have made a difference. Who knows what would have happened if I'd had a real relationship with Rick Maloney beyond a few postcards over the years? Instead, I had you, Max, Coop and Damon."

Linc gritted his teeth as he thought about the random and infrequent postcards Rick had sent when they were younger. It almost added insult to injury to think their father could find the time to mail a few lines but not be a meaningful part of any of their lives. Then he smiled at his baby sister. "You turned out great despite us."

"Such a comedian," Justine said. "It's okay to take a compliment, Linc. Everyone knows you're a hard worker and responsible, but you have a big heart, too. You just hide it behind all that practicality."

"Unlike our brothers—the trio of terror—you were an easy kid, Justine. I didn't have to do much to help with you."

"But you did," she countered. "I remember the times you sat with me at the table making dioramas or working on math homework when Mom was too tired. Most teenage boys would have ignored their baby sister. You made me feel like I had someone looking out for me."

Linc felt heat rise to his cheeks. He wasn't sure how to handle this spontaneous love fest from his sister. It certainly wasn't what he'd expected when he came to see her today. "I like dioramas," Linc told her with a smile.

"Okay, if you squirm any more you'll fall out of that seat." Justine held a cherry tomato aloft on her fork. "I'll stop with the Lincoln Fortune Maloney fan fest now." She popped the tomato into her mouth.

"Praise the Lord." Linc made a show of wiping his brow.

"All I'm saying is that if you find a woman to fall for, you've got plenty to offer her. You're not like Rick Maloney. You'd make a great dad."

Her eyes lit up as she looked past him. "Speaking of great dads, look who's here."

Linc turned and then stood to greet his brother-in-law. Stefan Mendoza was movie-star handsome with his tanned skin, close-cropped dark hair, and deep green eyes. He'd retained a bit of his Miami big-city polish, but the man only had eyes for Justine, much to Linc's relief.

Today Stefan wore dark gray slacks, a linen button-down, and held in his arms his fifteen-month-old son, Linc's nephew, Morgan. The baby babbled with happiness at the sight of his mother, then turned to eye Linc with an assessing stare.

The kid clearly hadn't gotten the message from his mom about what a prize catch his uncle was.

"Hello to my two best guys." Justine kissed Stefan on the cheek before lifting Morgan into her arms.

"Hope we're not interrupting serious Maloney family business," Stefan said with an easy smile. "I wanted to stop by and say hi."

"Plenty of fries to go around." Linc gestured to an empty chair. "Please join us. My sister has been telling me how blissfully happy she is as a married woman. I'm sure her other brothers will be just as happy as me to hear it. I feel like I should buy you a beer, especially now that you're the expert."

Stefan chuckled. "Save the drink for a time when we're relaxing together and I'm not on my way to a meeting. Besides, keeping Justine happy is my great honor and privilege."

The newlyweds shared a look that made Linc's chest pull tight in what felt like jealousy. Impossible. He didn't want the kind of domestic bliss his sister had found.

"So what's new with our favorite multimillionaire?" Stefan asked. "Is living the life of leisure boring you half to death yet?"

"I'm finding ways to entertain myself," Linc answered. He didn't want to admit how close his sister's husband had come to the truth. He certainly wasn't about to share the extent of his late-night online shopping adventures with a man like Stefan. The latter had a great career and seemed to embody everything Linc no longer associated with himself. He was a hardworking man with lots going on in his life.

But Stefan possessed more than Linc ever had because he managed to balance his work with being an excellent family man. Linc was happy for Justine and Stefan. Not jealous, he told himself. No need for jealousy.

"What does a person do with that amount of sudden wealth?" Stefan sounded genuinely curious. "Are you looking at investment opportunities or new career adventures?"

Linc nodded. "A little of both." It wasn't exactly a lie. "I'm taking things slow, so I find the right fit. Just because I have a lot of money doesn't mean I want to waste it."

What a complete fabrication when he thought of all the useless spending he'd done.

The answer satisfied Stefan, who nodded. "Makes sense. From everything your sister says, I have no doubt you'll do right by the Fortune name and your grandfather's legacy."

Linc didn't try to hold back his scoff. "My grandfather didn't bother to take part in our lives when we were younger." He tried and most likely failed to keep the bitterness from his voice. "I'm not concerned about honoring his legacy. My focus is taking advantage of the new opportunities this money affords me."

"You deserve to have some fun with it, too," Justine said, sounding like a loyal younger sister.

"I understand. But now you have an opportunity to create your own legacy," Stefan countered.

Linc didn't quite know how to react to the idea of that.

"You should hold your nephew," Justine suggested as if she knew it was time to steer the conversation to topics that might include less emotional land mines.

Linc wasn't sure holding a toddler would do the trick, but he appreciated the effort just the same.

Before he had a chance to protest, his sister moved around the table and deposited Morgan into his arms. The boy stared up at him with wide eyes before breaking into a toothy grin.

Linc didn't have much firsthand experience with babies or toddlers. Sure, he'd seen them come into GreatStore over the years, but he wasn't the kind of guy to make a big fuss or ooh and aah over a cute kid.

Holding Morgan made him question why he'd chosen to keep his distance from kids in the first place.

He liked holding his nephew. A lot. He'd met Morgan a few times, but there were always so many people who wanted to hold the kid so Linc had kept his distance.

Now he noticed Morgan smelled like lavender and pears, a strange combination but one that was strangely intoxicating. Then there was the warmth and weight of him, which felt perfectly balanced in Linc's arms.

He was holding an actual human, one who was soft and kind of fidgety, breathing out rapid puffs of air that warmed Linc's jaw.

Also, his nephew trained those big eyes on Linc like he could see into the very depths of his uncle's soul.

Linc hadn't spared a thought about his soul until this very moment.

"I'm starting to freak him out," he muttered, darting a panicked glance first at Justine and then Stefan. "His chin is wobbly. He's going to cry."

"Give it a minute," Justine said in a universal mom voice. "He needs to get used to you."

"He can do that from across the table. Maybe he wants to walk around. I could be cramping his style. I don't want—"

The boy smiled again.

"Oh. Well, that's better."

"I told you so." Justine sat down across from Linc.

"You're a natural," Stefan added.

"I don't think so." Linc stared at the toddler, who

stared and patted a hand against Linc's cheek before letting out a long sigh.

"He's sleepy," Justine explained.

"Aren't babies supposed to fuss when they're tired?" Linc started to bounce the little guy the way he'd seen Stefan doing when they walked in.

"Morgan isn't often fussy." Stefan took his wife's hand and squeezed it. "We're lucky."

"In so many ways," Justine agreed.

And just like that, Linc's world tipped on its axis. He'd never thought of himself as possessing potential as a dad. Still, he reminded himself, just because he enjoyed holding a kid for a few minutes, that did not make him father material.

He remembered Rick holding Damon while standing in the kitchen talking to Kimberly. Linc would sit at the table doing homework while Max and Cooper played cars or built toy log houses on the living room floor.

Rick had always been lifting one or another boy— sometimes two at a time—into his arms. He'd never given any indication that he wanted a life other than the one he had, at least not that Linc noticed.

Not until the day he'd left.

So what if Linc liked holding a baby? What did it matter if he could imagine Remi's dark eyes and sweet smile on a tiny child's face?

That wouldn't guarantee Linc's ability to commit. Liking kids didn't make a person a good father.

Sticking around and doing the work when things got hard made someone a decent parent.

Mistakes were okay, but leaving was a coward's way out, and Linc wasn't convinced he would stay.

He finished the lunch with Justine and Stefan, his brother-in-law polishing off most of Linc's sandwich. The visit had squashed Linc's appetite.

He didn't make a big deal of holding Morgan because what kind of loser would he be if he couldn't deal with a baby for fifteen minutes. But as soon as they finished, he gratefully returned his nephew to the boy's mother.

As they walked out of the hotel, Stefan mentioned a few of the other newer businesses in Rambling Rose, all of which had been developed or were owned by a member of the Fortune family.

Linc certainly had the money to make a significant impact in his community, but in what way?

He didn't have a burning desire to open a restaurant or spa. A hotel seemed like far more of an investment than he could take on by himself.

Maybe he and his brothers could come up with a plan of action once they each received their inheritance. The thought of finding something that would give all of them equal purpose seemed like a Herculean task.

He hugged his sister, dropped a kiss on his nephew's sweetly scented head and shook Stefan's hand. The trio headed in the opposite direction and Linc was once again caught off guard by the pang of jealousy that stabbed through his chest.

He didn't want what his sister had, he reminded himself as he headed toward his car.

He liked his simple life. Or so he told himself.

Somehow that mantra no longer rang true.

He decided to stop downtown for a coffee before heading back and found a parking spot in front of Kirby's Perks. As he hit the lock button on the Ferrari's key fob, he noticed an older man exiting the shop.

"Martin," Linc called with a wave.

Martin Smith's eyes widened in apparent surprise, then he waved in return.

"Lincoln, hello." He gestured toward the sports car. "I noticed this beauty while having my midday coffee and wondered who it belonged to. Not exactly a subtle choice, son."

Linc shrugged. "There was nothing subtle about that check you gave me."

Martin drew in a long, almost labored breath as he considered that. "How's the adjustment period going? From what I've heard, you've only recently begun to live like a man of means."

"Are you keeping tabs on me?"

"I care about you and your family," Martin answered. "Your grandfather would have wanted to know you were happy."

"I'm sure Wendell Fortune would have agreed that money can't buy happiness."

"Yes." Martin nodded. "You're right about that.

So how are you, Lincoln? What brings you to Rambling Rose?"

"I drove down to have lunch with my sister. Stefan brought Morgan by the restaurant as well."

"Adorable lad. I didn't realize how much I liked babies until Morgan came along."

"He's a cute kid," Linc agreed, not wanting to share how much he related to Martin's sentiment.

"Your sister is happy, and it had nothing to do with money."

"Yeah, it's nice to see Justine that way."

"And you?" Martin prompted.

"No complaints," Linc said automatically. "What would I have to complain about?"

Martin chuckled. "Your grandfather might have given you some ideas. He found living the life of a wealthy man to be quite the burden at times."

Linc frowned. "Is that why he disappeared?"

"Probably," Martin said with a shrug. "He was a simple man."

"Yeah." Linc clenched his fist around the key fob as an unwelcome comparison between himself and the grandfather he never knew entered his mind. "Apparently, it was easier to pretend he had no family and no responsibilities than to stand up and do the right thing. Just like his own son."

"Wendell had regrets about some of his choices." Martin frowned at the car. "I'm sure he'd want to know his inheritance is helping to rectify some of the mistakes he made."

"If Wendell wanted things simple, then he'd be disappointed in the outcome." Linc dragged a hand through his hair. "Money makes spending it simpler, but it complicates many other things."

"Not the important things," Martin countered, tugging at the end of his bushy beard.

Linc opened his mouth to argue, then closed it. Maybe the older man had a point.

"Any chance you can give me an inkling as to when Max will be getting his money? I think my brothers are starting to wonder if they'll get a chance to experience the wealthy man's life for themselves."

Martin inclined his head. "The money is coming in due time. It's good to know that the change in your financial status hasn't changed who you are as a man, Linc." He grinned, then took a sip of his coffee. "I mean, other than a flashy new ride."

"Thanks, I think. My brothers would tell you I'm still a boring stick-in-the-mud."

"Your grandfather would be proud of you." Martin coughed like the words had choked him up.

"You two really were close."

The old man nodded and rolled his lips together.

"I appreciate what you're doing for us, Martin. Helping Wendell like you are."

"I'd do anything for you, Justine and your brothers," Martin said, his voice husky.

It was a strange comment from a man who was basically the executor of Wendell Fortune's will.

Before Linc had a chance to question him on the

emotional outburst, a woman leaned out the front door of the coffee shop and called to Martin.

"I'll talk to you soon," the old man told Linc. After a hearty pat on Linc's shoulder, Martin turned and walked away.

Linc climbed into the Ferrari and sped away from Rambling Rose, grateful to be returning to his simple life, although the visit had left him with more questions than answers.

Chapter Sixteen

"Are you going to tell him today?"

Remi's hand stilled on the thermos of coffee she'd just poured. She turned to face her mother. "I haven't decided on the job offer yet, so there's nothing to tell."

Stella pulled her robe more tightly closed and re-tied the belt as she walked into the kitchen. "I wasn't talking about the potential job or you possibly moving away from Chatelaine." She pulled a mug from one of the upper cabinets. "Are you going to tell Lincoln that you're in love with him?"

Remi scoffed as she watched her mother pour coffee into the mug adorned with hummingbirds and then add a generous splash of cream.

"Old news. Everyone other than Linc has known about my crush on him for years. Honestly, I thought

I was hiding my feelings better. But I don't see any reason to mention it to him at this point."

Stella turned and studied Remi as she raised the mug to her mouth and sipped. "Maybe it started as a crush, but it's more than that now, sweetheart. We both know it."

Remi blinked. "I don't know anything of the sort," she lied but shouldn't have bothered.

One delicate arch of her mother's brow had her throwing up her hands and letting out a mock scream. "Okay, I love him. Truly, madly, deeply, and all the rest. I tried not to. I tried my hardest. I don't want it." She squeezed shut her eyes. "Oh, Mom. What am I going to do now?"

"Tell him," Stella urged gently, taking Remi's hand in hers. "You should tell him how you feel."

"That's a horrible idea," Remi said, dashing her free hand across her cheeks. "It's the worst idea ever. I would rather dip my toes in boiling lava or toss my body into the fires of Mount Doom or face down He Who Must Not Be Named with only my lightning scar to protect me. Any of those feels like a better alternative to admitting to Linc that I love him."

Her mother's lips twitched, although she managed to keep her features neutral. "Do you think you're being a tad dramatic, my girl?"

"No. The options I just mentioned involve pain in my body. I could tolerate physical pain, although the burning fires of a volcano might be pushing it a little. If I tell Linc how I feel and he reacts badly, my heart will be destroyed. I've never given my heart to someone."

"I know," Stella said, her smile gentle. "Your heart is precious. It's special. I understand that it would hurt if Linc didn't reciprocate your feelings, but you'll never know if you don't share how you feel."

Remi placed a thermos of coffee in the insulated picnic bag she was packing for the boating expedition today.

"I subscribe to the belief that ignorance is bliss." She moved to the refrigerator to load the sandwiches and a container of fresh cut fruit she'd prepared into the bag.

"I don't believe that." Stella took a seat at the table, coffee mug cradled in her hands. "No one as dedicated to books and knowledge as you would believe that ignorance is best."

"I can pretend."

"You're going to have to tell him at some point. What if you decide to take the job in San Antonio? Don't you think he'll realize you're gone?"

"Of course, I'll tell him if I take the job. I'm not sure if you've noticed, but Linc has a lot of time on his hands. There's no reason we couldn't continue just the way things are, only we'll do it from a distance."

"You deserve better. That's the reason you can't continue this way. I know how big your heart is, Remi. I know how much you have to offer someone and what it must cost you to hold back. Let Linc in.

Let him see how much you have to offer and what he'd be missing without you."

Remi felt her grip tighten on the refrigerator door. As much as she wanted to, she didn't bother to deny her mother's assessment of the situation. "Our current situation is not ideal," she admitted. "But it's better than losing him completely."

She glanced at the clock above the sink. "Mom, I can't talk about this anymore. He'll be here any minute, and I'll be choking back tears if I don't pull myself together." She closed the door and finished packing the bag with crackers and the cookies she'd baked last night.

When Linc called to tell her he'd picked up the boat the previous morning and invited her to spend the day on Lake Chatelaine with him, he'd explained that it was just going to be the two of them. Paul, Alec and Alana were all working.

Linc wanted a chance to get familiar with his new boat before bringing his friends aboard. She hadn't questioned his reasoning, although part of her head secretly hoped he also wanted some time with her. They spent nearly every evening together. Linc might not tell her he cared for her, but he made her feel cherished with his actions.

Remi didn't want to believe she was settling, but she also wanted a love like her parents had. They'd had so many years of devotion along with a healthy dose of mutual respect and patience. Her father would never have allowed her mother to feel uncertain about his love. He'd hate to know his daughter was letting fear run her life.

"I'll tell him when I decide on the job." She zipped the bag and faced her mother. "If I decide to leave Chatelaine, then I'll let him know that the only way our relationship can continue is if he can commit to me. You're right, Mom. I deserve that. I don't want to put pressure on him, but I can't keep going on this way."

Her mother gave a slight nod. "And what if you decide to stay, which you know would be my preference?"

Remi thought for a moment, then shrugged. "Even if I stay in Chatelaine. Linc needs to decide what he wants. If it's me, I need more than this uncertainty."

She glanced out the window that looked over the front yard. His headlights lit up the lawn as he pulled to a stop at the curb, the boat trailered behind his old truck.

"Go enjoy yourself today," Stella told her. "Things are going to work out for you, sweetheart. You are a fantastic person with a good heart. You deserve to be happy, and I'm not just saying that because I'm your mama."

Remi gave Stella a quick hug as she walked past the table. "I appreciate that. I'll see you later, Mom."

"Did you pack sunscreen?"

Remi grinned. "Of course. You taught me well."

She grabbed the food bag and the backpack that held her extra clothes, then headed out the front door.

The light was beginning to dawn in the eastern sky. She stowed her bags in the back seat and climbed in next to Linc.

"I know your dad was an avid fisherman," he said as she buckled her seat belt. "I hope we can do him proud."

She pretended to consider that. "I don't know about your skills casting a line, but there's no doubt I inherited my father's propensity to be a fish whisperer."

"I like your confidence." Linc leaned across the console to kiss her. "I like everything about you."

The now-familiar tingles that always accompanied his kisses washed through her. Maybe her mom was right, and she had nothing to worry about.

Maybe Linc was being patient for her sake. No man looked at a woman the way he looked at her if he didn't feel something serious.

She had to have faith. Just as her mom predicted, everything would work out the way it was meant to.

They started toward the lake, and Remi was content to watch their quiet town roll by in the muted light of morning. She usually rose early for her shifts at the store but rarely took time to appreciate how peaceful things appeared during this sleepy hour.

"I finished *Pride and Prejudice* last night," Linc told her, reaching across the console to place a hand on her jeans-clad leg.

He wore cargo pants and a long-sleeve performance hoodie. With the shadow of stubble darkening his jaw and his rumpled hair curling under the bill of a Texas Tech baseball cap, he looked like the kind of man to whom Jane Austen would have given her approval. If someone transported him to Regency England, that is.

"I didn't like Darcy as well as Captain Wentworth from *Persuasion*, although he was certainly better than that Wickham guy."

"That Wickham guy," she repeated on a puff of shocked air. "You've read both *Pride and Prejudice* and *Persuasion*?"

He gave her a sidelong glance and shrugged. "It shouldn't come as a shock. I have plenty of time on my hands. You told me I should read the books before we watch the movies, so I'm making my way through them. I missed having a mystery or thriller element, but she's a good writer."

"Jane Austen is definitely a good writer," Remi agreed and bit down on the inside of her cheek to keep from blurting out that she was in love with him. How could she help fall in love with a guy who read Jane Austen?

"I brought you a cinnamon roll," he said like it was no big deal.

"Now you're not playing fair," she told him, and he chuckled like he couldn't understand what she meant.

He reached into the back seat with one hand and then placed a brown paper bag in her lap. "Hope you like it."

She peered at the creamy, gooey-looking pastry and turned to Linc. "Did you bake this? Because I'm pretty sure there's no place in Chatelaine to get a cinnamon roll that looks this good. You can't beat the Tumbleweed Diner's pancakes but nobody does cinnamon rolls like that."

"Would you believe me if I told you I did?"

"Not a chance."

He entered the marina parking lot and put the truck into park as she pulled the cinnamon roll from the bag. "You're too smart for your own good." Leaning over, he scooped a smidge of icing onto the tip of his finger, licked it off, then kissed her, now tasting of toothpaste mixed with vanilla frosting.

The day was already perfect.

Remi remembered mornings on the lake with her father. They often started with muttered curses as he tried to maneuver their small boat into the water from the concrete ramp. There wasn't much to the public access area just like there hadn't been much to her father's boat.

Linc's boat was much bigger and probably cost ten times what her father's had, but he showed immense patience as the two of them figured out the best way to launch it. Because it was late January and a weekday morning, not to mention the fact that they started from the private LC Club marina where many of the boats had been shrink wrapped and dry docked for the season, the lake was virtually empty and very peaceful.

Even so, the marina was impressive and well-maintained. LC Club members had a private mechanic and a snack bar that would open for the summer season. Her dad would have gotten a kick out the way the fancy folks lived, although she doubted he would have been jealous. He'd had been happy with his life just the way it was. Remi felt that way this morning.

Once the boat was in the water and the truck and trailer parked for the day, they took off. She sat on the boat's bow as Linc sped across the glassy water.

A hawk dove from one of the trees surrounding the lake and then emerged from the water clutching a silvery fish in his sharp talons. The sight of so much predatory beauty took her breath away.

Eventually, Linc cut the motor as they turned the corner toward a small inlet. "I was talking to one of the guys in the GreatStore tackle department. He told me this was the best place to fish."

She grinned. "It was my father's favorite spot."

"Then it must be perfect." He drew her in closer for another sweet kiss.

"Are you trying to distract me so that I'll be off my fishing game?" she asked as she pushed against his chest.

"How do you already know me so well?" he shot back with a wink.

They got out the fishing gear and positioned themselves on opposite sides of the boat to cast. It had been years since Remi had been fishing, but it all came back to her, along with so many precious memories of relaxing days spent with her father. She wished he'd gotten to know Linc and had a feeling the two men would have bonded immediately.

They fished and later explored every corner of Lake Chatelaine. There were several times that Remi came close to sharing her job offer, but something made her hold back.

Otherwise, the day remained as perfect as it had started. When he invited her to his house after for dinner and a movie—Jane Austen no less—there was no question in her mind about agreeing. She knew in her heart she would always say yes when it came to this man.

Later that night, Linc's heart pounded as he stared up at the shadowy ceiling above him. It wasn't real, he reminded himself.

Although the nightmare he'd just woken from certainly felt authentic enough.

He absently touched the ring finger of his left hand and swallowed back a cry of relief when he found it still bare.

He could hear Remi's even breathing next to him in bed. She slept soundly, unaware of the panic coursing through Linc.

There was no reason to associate her with the disturbing dream.

Of course she'd spent the night. He'd invited her to stay. It wasn't like he regretted it.

He had no regrets when it came to this woman, although the dream that had rocked his world continued to feel so real.

Even now, he could see him and Remi together in his house—their house.

There had been children, so many children. An army of little ones.

The babies might have been adorable, just like his nephew, Morgan, but it was hard to tell with all the crying.

He and Remi shared the house as a married couple in the dream, but she'd been out. He was there alone with the crying babies and toddlers he found impossible to comfort.

He'd been holding a child in each arm, but that wasn't all. There'd been more kids in highchairs and strollers positioned around the house. Dozens of babies he could do nothing to pacify. He'd wanted to, but it was as if his mouth were taped shut. His limbs weighed a thousand pounds and refused to obey when he commanded them to move. Then the door opened, and even in his dream, the sense of relief Linc felt overwhelmed him.

It had to be Remi coming to rescue him. Coming to save their children—why did they have so many children—from him because he was clearly incapable of managing independently.

Only it hadn't been Remi. Rick Maloney stood in the doorway, surveying the chaos surrounding Linc, a slight smirk on his face. Linc's father hadn't offered a single word of encouragement. He also hadn't aged. He looked exactly as he had in Linc's memory from that final day in the yard.

Rick's sandy-blond hair boyishly curled over one eye, and his gaze had the look of a man who was worn out by life. Linc's eyes were the same color as his dad's, and he wondered if dream Linc had the same exhausted, somewhat panicked look in their depths.

He called for help over the wailing, unsure whether the noise drowned out his voice or if his father simply chose to ignore him.

Rick shook his head before he turned and walked away. Linc tried to take a step forward at that point, but one of the babies he held—a little girl—began to slip from his grasp. He tried to adjust his arm to pull her in tight, but she continued to fall. And just as she hit the ground was the moment he woke up.

He'd been lying there awake for almost ten minutes but still struggled to calm his thundering heart.

Remi shifted in her sleep, shifting closer and reaching out as if to comfort him.

Of course she would sense he needed it. She was perfect. Beautiful and pure.

She would never falter, even with a dozen kids clamoring for her attention. He wanted to be a man who deserved her. He wanted a future with this woman despite denying it to himself and her for so long.

But how could he reach for that when he couldn't even handle dream children?

He forced his mind back to the present moment, trying to dispel his dream failure from his consciousness. A dream, he reminded himself. Nothing more.

Nothing because he wouldn't let it become more.

When the first light of dawn peeked through the curtain's edge, Linc got out of bed without a sound and made his way to the kitchen. He had omelets, hash browns and a bowl of fresh-cut fruit that would have fed a half dozen people ready when Remi woke.

She took in his handiwork as she entered the kitchen. "To what do I owe this frenzy of culinary effort?" she asked, taking a long sip from the mug of coffee he handed her.

"I thought you'd enjoy it." He hoped his smile didn't look as wooden as it felt. It was a dream, he reminded himself again. She had given him no indication that she wanted to settle down or have a million kids running around.

There was no reason for him to assume they couldn't continue with their casual relationship just the way it was. Yes, if he had to choose a woman for a commitment, Remi would be his first and only pick.

But he didn't want commitment.

He couldn't handle commitment even if he did want it. The dream had brought to the surface his greatest fear, and he needed to pay attention to that.

"Are you okay?" she asked, studying him. "Did you just tell me to pay attention to something?"

He grimaced, not realizing he'd spoken the words

out loud. "Too much coffee. Have a seat. Let's have breakfast, and then I'll take you home."

"Oh, okay." She slid into the seat, and he told himself not to freak out any more than he was. It was breakfast. There was nothing to be worried about. Breakfast only meant breakfast. At least he could handle that.

Chapter Seventeen

Remi didn't know how she'd managed to make it through the awkward, tense meal with Linc and not give herself away. He was acting so strange.

Although she knew nothing had changed from the previous night, when he'd held her in his arms so tenderly, to this morning when he could barely make eye contact with her, she couldn't help but think about what had caused this shift in him.

Had he received a text or phone call this morning that somehow made him know she was keeping her potential plans from him?

She didn't like feeling as though she were deceiving him, but every time she opened her mouth to reveal the whole situation, the words seemed to lodge in her throat. She was being silly. They'd had the best day. She'd had the best few weeks of her life with Linc.

But yesterday on the boat had reminded her so much of the special times she'd shared with her dad. Remi had come back to Chatelaine to help her mom after her father died because she knew it was what he would have wanted.

What he'd want her to do now was be brave enough to admit her feelings to Linc, consequences be damned.

She waited until he pulled into her mother's driveway, the Ferrari engine idling with a soothing purr.

"I had a great time," he said and patted her knee with a little too much force, so very different from the way he'd touched her the previous day.

It almost made her lose her nerve. Almost. "There's something I've been meaning to tell you," she said. "It's about the future."

"That's what I appreciate most about us, Rem." He smiled, if it could be called a smile. She would describe it more as a grimace. "We don't have to worry about things like the future. We can have fun."

"Yes." She tugged at the end of her ponytail. "Fun. You know what isn't fun?"

"Pressure," Linc muttered.

"GreatStore closing the book section," she blurted. "Me moving to San Antonio for a new job."

Linc went pale as he gaped at her. "What are you talking about? Why would GreatStore close the book section?"

"To make more room for Electronics."

"And why would you move to San Antonio?"

"For a new job working in a bookstore."

The words were difficult to say, but she felt a lightness enter her chest. It was good to tell him her truth, and she knew she needed to be completely honest.

"Why?"

"Because I don't know that I want to sell tablets and headphones."

"You want to move?"

"No," she told him honestly, then swallowed and added, "I want you to give me a reason to stay."

He stared at her so long that Remi felt herself begin to squirm. But she was being brave for herself. To honor her father's memory and make her mother proud.

"I've had so much fun with you lately, Linc. You've been the best part of this new year for me, but I can't keep going like this."

"Don't, Remi," he whispered so softly she barely heard him. But she did.

Still, she refused to stop.

"I'm in love with you, Linc. Not because of the money or what we've done. What's fun to me is the two of us together. I want more of us, but not only casually. I'm not that kind of a person."

"So you're just going to leave?"

"I don't want to, but I need more. I need commitment. I know it scares you, but you aren't your dad. You're a good man. The kind of man I'd like to build a life with."

Linc shook his head. "We agreed to have fun."

"I want more," she repeated and tugged at her sweatshirt, wishing she was wrapped in enough protective layers to keep her safe from the heartbreak she could feel heading toward her like a runaway train. She held up a hand when he would have spoken. "I know I've shocked you. Don't say anything. Just know that I believe in you. In us."

"You shouldn't," he said, gripping the steering wheel like it was all he had to ground him to this world. "I mean, I can't... I don't... I wasn't expecting this. You know I care about you, right?"

She nodded, trying not to let her sadness show. She'd surprised him. She didn't have a reason to worry yet. He looked shocked, not disgusted. Of course it would be a shock for him.

She needed to tell him what was in her heart for both their sakes. Luckily, her brain was still functioning, and she knew what she needed most of all was to get herself out of this situation.

"Take some time, Linc." A pause before he said something both of them might regret. "I know it's a surprise, but it will make sense if you give it a chance. We make sense. I don't want to lose you. But don't answer now." She sounded like a babbling fool.

"How long have you known?" The question was spoken barely above a whisper.

Her chest tightened. In truth, she'd been in love

with him for years. Only recently had it become so apparent that she couldn't ignore her feelings any longer.

He flicked his gaze toward her when she didn't immediately answer. "Do Paul and Alec know about the book department as well?"

Okay, so this wasn't about her heart. It was about the store. Maybe it was a safer topic. "I've known for a couple of weeks. I'm not sure about Alec. Paul is the one who told me, but I asked him not to say anything until I figured out what I wanted to do."

"You wanted to leave Chatelaine without discussing it with me? Without telling me what you were thinking beforehand?"

She blinked. "I'm telling you right now."

His brows furrowed. "But you knew. You were making plans without me."

"I didn't want you to feel pressured. I wanted to take care of my future."

She didn't understand his reaction, but this wasn't how she wanted the conversation to go.

"Did you even try to think of another solution?" he demanded. "You're just going to walk away?"

"I'm not walking away," she said quietly. "But I need a reason to stay."

He opened his mouth and shut it again, along with his eyes, which was for the best. She didn't want him to see her struggle to hold it together.

"I'm going to go inside," she said, her voice shaky.

"We both have a lot to think about. I love you, Linc. That's most important, at least to me."

When he still didn't speak, she felt tears gather behind her eyes. She got out of the car and hurried up the walk to her mother's house.

"Why didn't you tell me? Friends don't keep secrets."

Later that afternoon, Paul looked up from his computer as Linc stormed into the GreatStore back office. "Dude, calm down. Remi asked me not to say anything for a little while."

"Your loyalty is suddenly with her? I thought we were friends."

"You know we're friends. This isn't about loyalty. I didn't tell anyone when you spent months staring at the balance of your bank account without spending it. I was being respectful to her."

"By disrespecting me. By betraying me." Linc knew he sounded like a world-class jerk but couldn't stop the anger coursing through him. "I should have known, Paul."

"It wasn't my business to tell you." His friend pushed back from the desk and crossed his arms over his chest. "I don't appreciate you charging in here like you own the place. You might have the money to buy half this town, but you don't own me. I'm getting a little tired of you acting like you do, and I'm not the only one."

Linc took a step back as shock reverberated through

him like a splash of cold water on his temper. "That's what you think I'm doing?"

Paul's gaze was heated. "Alec and I were your friends long before you were rich, Linc. I'm happy for you. We both are, but lately things feel different. You don't have to pick up the tab or arrange elaborate activities. I don't know who you're trying to impress with all of your late-night spending, but we like you already. I'm your friend, not part of your entourage."

Linc couldn't help but laugh at that. "I'm not cool enough to have an entourage."

"Exactly. It's about time you realized it."

His friend's words were similar to what Remi had told him, and Linc was once again reminded that he'd had a good life with great friends before the inheritance. He didn't need to let the money rule his life or change how he related to the people he cared about.

"I guess I don't have a choice since you're around to keep me grounded. I appreciate it." He blew out a breath. "Although, I still wish someone would have told me earlier about them eliminating the book department. Maybe I could have done something to help. I still could. I'm friends with a lot of people at corporate."

"You don't work here anymore," Paul pointed out, unnecessarily in Linc's opinion. "I think Remi wanted to figure out her feelings about the change before she talked to anyone. By the way, I have friends at corporate, too. I've made a case for shrinking the

book section but not eliminating it completely. Unfortunately—"

"It doesn't need to be shrunk or eliminated. We
sell a lot of books in Chatelaine."

"There is no *we*. Once again, you don't work here."

"I still care."

"About books or Remi?"

"Both," Linc said through gritted teeth. "Did you
know she's thinking about moving to San Antonio?"

Paul nodded. "We discussed her job offer."

"Since when did the two of you become so close?"
Linc tried to unknot the ball of jealousy in his stomach. "Is there something I should know?"

"Remi and I are friends and coworkers." Paul
drew in a deep breath. "You know life has gone on
without you around here."

Ouch. More grounding. Just what Linc needed. He
was used to both Paul and Alec being lighthearted
and easygoing. They didn't take anything too seriously. At least that was Linc's impression.

"I'm well aware, and it seems to me that's how you
like it." Paul had been promoted after Linc left, and
until this moment, he hadn't given much thought to
what that would mean for his friend. "You've taken
over my job, and now you're keeping secrets for
Remi? Maybe there's something you'd like to share
with me."

"As a matter of fact." Paul rose from his chair
slowly and ran a hand through his cropped hair. He'd
always worn it long and shaggy, but it would seem

he was embodying his new role in management. "I'd like to share that you are being a complete knucklehead and that if you don't want to lose Remi, you should do something about it. Make an effort. Win her heart."

"You're giving me dating advice?" Linc felt as though he was in an emotional free fall. He'd been rock-steady his entire life, but he could not seem to reel in his anger and hurt, even if it was unwarranted. "That's rich. I don't need to talk to you—"

"You need to talk to Remi," Paul said, one thick brow lifted. "Tell her how you feel."

"I feel mad as hell," Linc shot back. "Do you think that's what she wants to hear?"

"I think that's what you're telling yourself because you're actually scared as hell. You like things easy, Linc. Relationships aren't easy."

"They can be. Mine have been."

"That was before."

"Before what?"

"Before you really got to know Remi."

"I've known her for years."

"Before you noticed her in that dress on New Year's Eve."

"The dress had nothing to do with it. She's beautiful in a pair of sweatpants."

"Were things simple before she pressured you to man up and admit you two aren't just doing the whole friends-with-benefits thing?"

"I respect her too much for that." Linc realized

his argument didn't hold weight in light of his recent behavior.

Apparently, so did Paul. "If you respect her, be honest with her and with yourself. It's okay to take a chance on something that might not work out."

"I thought I was taking a chance," he said, more to himself than Paul. "But she's willing to walk away. Maybe Remi's the one you should be giving this lecture to."

Paul gave a disgusted shake of his head. "I can't help a man who won't help himself."

"There's still a chance of saving the book department," Linc insisted. "I refuse to believe otherwise."

"Believe whatever you want," Paul told him. "Maybe along with your big checkbook, you have some sort of superhuman power over a giant, multinational company that the rest of us don't. I hope whatever you're planning makes a difference. Right now, I've got to get back to work."

Linc nodded. "We're still meeting up later for the game, right?"

Paul laughed. "You have more important things to sort out than a game, my friend." He walked past Linc with a pat on the shoulder that felt almost sympathetic.

Linc had things to sort out. Sure, he could do that. He was a problem solver. A solutions guy who'd been shouldering more than his share of responsibility since he was an eight-year-old kid.

Remi would understand. He could make her understand. He'd never lied to her or tried to deceive her about what he could and couldn't give.

He walked through the store, greeting old friends and noticing a few new faces.

It felt strange that he'd only been gone for a month and already there were members of the staff he didn't know.

He supposed it was to be expected. There was turnover even in a town like Chatelaine.

Although GreatStore had always been like a second home to him while he managed employees and moved through his days with a satisfying comfort level, the store was no longer his place.

He could buy all the fishing tackle or household accessories stocked on the GreatStore shelves. But he wasn't part of it the way he used to be, and no amount of movie nights or parties would stop that change.

Too many changes.

Linc ended up at the edge of the book department without even realizing it. He shouldn't have been surprised. Thinking back on it, he'd often found excuses for why he should check in with Remi when he'd been on staff.

Only now, instead of placing books on the shelves, she was taking them off, packing them into cardboard boxes and stacking them to one side of the aisle.

"It doesn't have to be this way," he said as he approached.

Her initial reaction to seeing him was a smile that

warmed him all the way to his toes. Then her gaze turned guarded, and it was like a cold gust of air blew in his direction.

"I didn't expect to see you here," she said.

"I wish you had told me sooner."

She glanced around as if to make sure no one was in earshot. "Which part, Linc? The change at the store or the truth in my heart?"

He thought back to their conversation in the car early that morning. He hadn't allowed himself to overthink what she'd revealed about her feelings for him. It was easier to focus on the perceived betrayal—the lie of omission.

How could she claim to be in love with him and not share something as crucial as potentially moving to a different city?

"I don't want you to leave Chatelaine," he said, hoping that would be enough.

"I know." She offered him a smile, but it wasn't reassuring. "You'll be fine. You have lots of adventures in front of you."

"What if I said I wanted to have those adventures with you?"

She bit down on her lower lip. "Is that what you're saying?"

"Why do we have to put labels on this? We had an agreement."

She slowly placed another stack of books into a box, then straightened and moved toward him. "We had no agreement."

"An understanding," he clarified, then took a step back as she continued to approach. Something in her gaze gave him pause and told him that retreat was the smartest choice he could make in this moment.

"I understand. You don't want to let me go, but you won't take a chance on us."

"I took you to California. Most women would be grateful for an all-expenses-paid trip. We've had fun together."

"I should be grateful that you're spending time with me?" she asked slowly.

"That isn't what I meant."

"It's what it sounded like," a voice said from nearby. Linc glanced over his shoulder to see Alana standing with Alec and several other staff members. All of them seemed to be glaring at him.

Alec shook his head and silently told Linc to cut off the conversation by sliding his finger across his throat. Linc ignored the signal. He might be messing up everything, and now he was doing it with an audience.

"Our deal was to have fun," he said, turning back to Remi.

"Then why did you get so mad about me not sharing the news about the book department?" She gestured to the half-empty row of shelves.

"Because we're friends."

"I thought we were more."

"You deserve more," Alana called out, placing her hands on her hips.

Linc shot her a narrow-eyed look, feeling heat creep up his neck. "Can we go someplace private to talk?"

Remi shook her head. "I have work to do."

"Before you leave town?"

Her chin trembled, and he wanted to pull her close. "I've told Paul I'm going to give it two weeks working in Electronics. The bookstore in San Antonio is willing to wait for my decision." Her eyes narrowed slightly. "They value me."

That was a jab at him, but he couldn't figure out why. He valued her. As a friend. As someone he had fun with. Didn't she understand he wasn't capable of giving more?

"Maybe because you were honest with them from the start."

He heard someone groan from the peanut gallery watching this scene unfold, but Linc didn't turn around. There was no reason to. Everything he needed to see was written on Remi's face.

"I'm sorry I didn't tell you about the book department right away." She looked at the floor, then up at him again, sorrow clouding her eyes. "But I'm not sorry I told you what's in my heart. You're right about honesty even if you can't—or won't—reciprocate. It's important even when it's difficult."

"Remi—"

"I need to get back to work, Linc. I think we've said all we have to say to each other."

No. He hadn't said any of the things he wanted to

tell her. But he still didn't have the words to make this right.

She watched him for another moment and then turned away with a sigh.

If Linc believed he had a heart to give, he would have felt it breaking as he walked away from Remi.

Chapter Eighteen

Remi shoved her spoon into the carton of butter brickle ice cream she'd purchased on her way out of the store after her shift that afternoon. She was scrolling through the channels and finding nothing of interest, when she heard the doorbell of her mother's house.

Her breath caught. She had no reason to believe Linc would stop by after how they'd left things earlier. She'd managed to keep herself busy for the rest of the afternoon, avoiding Alana, Paul and Alec and trying not to make eye contact with any of her other coworkers.

Only a few had witnessed the scene with Linc, but she knew word traveled fast. She didn't relish being the object of GreatStore staff gossip.

"Honey, will you get the door?" her mother called

from upstairs. "That's my ride to book club. There's still time for you to change your mind and join us."

If the idea of being scrutinized by her coworkers terrified Remi, the idea of facing her mother's nosy—if well-meaning—book club was a bit more than she could reasonably handle at the moment.

She dutifully padded toward the front door and opened it to find Kimberly Maloney smiling at her from the other side.

"Come on in," Remi offered, hoping she hid her emotions and didn't have ice cream dribbling down her shirt front. There was a chance Kimberly didn't yet know about the breakup with Linc. Not that they'd ever officially been dating.

If heartache was the yardstick by which a person measured the demise of a relationship, ending things with Linc was a breakup for the ages.

Kimberly patted Remi's arm as she followed her into the house.

"I'm guessing my son is to blame for you choosing ice cream as a main course tonight?"

Remi cringed. "It's not really Linc's fault," she said. "I can at least take responsibility for my poor food choices. For the record, this is just the appetizer. I might open a bag of cheese doodles later."

Kimberly offered a sympathetic smile. "I'm sorry the two of you are going through a rough patch."

"Is that how he described it?" Remi asked as she led Kimberly to the kitchen. She put the lid on the pint of ice cream before returning it to the freezer.

She could finish it later if she wanted to but chowing down with an audience was too much for her pride to take. She still had standards.

"I'm guessing you know Lincoln well enough to understand that he didn't tell me anything. But in Chatelaine word travels fast," Kimberly told her. "A friend of his sister's from high school was grocery shopping this afternoon, and she heard from someone who works at GreatStore that my son put on quite a show."

"We both contributed," Remi admitted. "I can't imagine he was any happier about a public scene than I was."

Kimberly inclined her head. "That friend called Justine, and Justine called me."

"I'm news for everyone in town." Remi shook her head. "Just what I always wanted."

"People care about you," Kimberly told her, "and Justine cares about her brother. Although thanks to the version she heard, I would say she's not Lincoln's biggest fan at the moment."

"Your son is a good man." It wasn't that Remi felt the need to defend Linc, but she spoke the truth from her heart. "I'm sure all of your sons are good men, but I'm talking about Linc."

Kimberly nodded. "I know. I also know he cares about you. But it's not easy for him to open himself to love."

"It's not easy for most of us," Remi answered.

"I know," Kimberly repeated. "I'm partly to blame for Linc's resistance."

"I would say his dad has more responsibility in that respect."

"Yes, but I let Linc grow up too soon. When Rick left, my world shattered. My heart, too, but who has time to worry about heartbreak when you're busy trying to take care of four rambunctious boys with a baby on the way?"

Remi blew out a breath. "I can't imagine."

"I didn't handle it well," Kimberly admitted. Her grip tightened on the strap of her patterned purse like she was drawing strength from the bag. "I tried, but I was embarrassed that my husband left me, and I didn't know how to manage on my own. So I allowed my eight-year-old son to become the man of the house. I realize now what a mistake that was. At the time, I was just grateful that Linc took on so much responsibility."

Remi's heart—as crushed as it was—ached for Kimberly's obvious regret and remorse. "I don't think Linc blames you for anything that happened when he was younger."

Kimberly nodded. "That's the worst part. For him, taking on responsibility became the norm. He didn't know anything else. And that…ugh…that girl he dated in high school hurt him because he tried to do the right thing for me and his siblings."

"Christine?" Remi had heard a few stories about

Linc and his ex-girlfriend, but he didn't like to talk about it.

"She broke up with him because he left college to help support his brothers and sister. Who does a thing like that?"

Remi shook her head, then paused. "You know that's not what I'm doing, right? I'm not walking away from my relationship with—"

"You're taking care of your heart," Kimberly said. "I hope my son is smart enough to understand his own heart before you leave."

"Who's leaving?" Stella asked as she walked into the kitchen, a hardback book tucked under her arm. "Didn't Remi tell you? She's decided to stay in Chatelaine."

Kimberly clasped her hands together. "Permanently? That's wonderful. But what about the job offer at the bookstore?"

Remi shrugged. "This is my home, even if I'm working in Electronics. I have ideas for improving the department, and I've reached out to the elementary school to discuss volunteering in their library. I'll find a way to share my love of books with people, even if I'm not running the book department." She smiled as her mother wrapped her in a tight hug.

"I'm so happy," Stella whispered.

"Me, too, Mom," Remi said, hoping that by saying the words out loud she'd start to believe them. "But I'm going to be moving out and finding my own place." She squeezed her mother's hand.

"That's exciting as well." Kimberly smiled. "A fresh start all the way around. Does Linc know about your decision?"

Remi shook her head. "I care about your son," she told the older woman. "I'm also in love with him. But I made this decision for me. I don't know what's going to happen with Linc, if anything. But I can take care of myself. And I want to be with a man who chooses me for me. Does that make sense?"

"It does," Kimberly told her. "Lincoln needs to figure out some things, but you should know that you make him a better person."

"I'm so proud of you, Remi," Stella said with another hug. "But now we need to get to book club before the ladies eat all the yummy appetizers I'm sure Sharla's going to provide."

"I hope that along with whatever your future holds, you still have time to give me book recommendations," Kimberly said. "The readers of this town appreciate you."

Remi's heart warmed at the woman's request. "It would be my great honor," she promised.

Linc sat in the Chatelaine Bar and Grill later that night and stared at the empty shot glass in front of him. "Bartender, another round."

"Big brother, I think you've had enough," Damon said, mimicking Linc's serious tone from behind the bar.

Linc shook his head. "Come on. Don't be a buzzkill. I even asked Max to give me a ride home later, so there's no reason I can't have one more."

Max, who sat on the stool next to Linc, dangled the keys to the Ferrari between two fingers. "You know Linc is desperate when he's agreed to let me drive the car."

"True enough. But it would be a shame to mess up all that Italian leather with puke," Damon said. He placed a glass of ice water in front of Linc.

"I'm not a puker," Linc promised, then realized he was slurring his words. "I never have been before."

"You've also never done four shots in less than an hour as far as I can remember."

"Do I need to take my business to a different bartender?"

His youngest brother laughed. "Good luck with that in Chatelaine."

Max patted him on the shoulder. "You're not going anywhere. We don't often see our practical, responsible, do-gooder big brother have a public meltdown. This is going to be way too much fun."

"I'm not having a public meltdown," Linc grumbled.

"That's right," Cooper agreed, taking a seat on Linc's other side. "Because you already did earlier today at GreatStore."

Linc scowled. "How did you hear—"

"Small town. Duh." Cooper waved away Linc's question. "You didn't expect your breakup with Remi to stay under wraps, right?"

"We didn't break up. We were never officially dating, so there was no official breakup."

"Bull," all three of his brothers said at once.

"Now you're giving me grief in stereo. I appreciate that so much. I should have stayed home. I could have gotten drunk and watched my new 5K television. My buzz hasn't even worn off, and you three are already giving me a headache."

"Whoa, a new television. Add it to the long list of your indiscriminate purchases. Is that supposed to make us jealous?" Damon asked with a chuckle.

"I'm not trying to make you jealous. Your money is coming. Each of you will eventually be in the same position I am right now."

"I don't think so." Max shook his head. "We're not going to be in the same position as you because— and I can only speak for myself—I don't have a best female friend that I'll be falling in love with any-time soon."

Linc had the sudden urge to stick out his tongue at his brother the way he'd done when he was a boy. "Love has nothing to do with it. This is about honesty."

Cooper tipped the beer bottle to his lips. "Okay, so let's talk about you not being honest with yourself regarding your feelings for Remi. The two of you are perfect for one another. You always have been. I don't understand why it's so hard for you to admit that."

"It doesn't matter how I feel about her. You three

know better than anyone why I can't be the man Remi needs and deserves."

His brothers continued to stare at him with similar expressions of bafflement on their faces. "I'm still on my first beer," Max said finally. "You're going to have to spell it out for me."

"I'm like Dad," Linc said, then sat back like he'd just done the ultimate mic drop. If that didn't explain to his brothers—

"No, you're not," Max told him. "Maybe you look like him, but that's it."

"Yes," Cooper agreed. "We all took something from him, but Rick Maloney was more of a sperm donor than any kind of real father."

"He was a father to me," Linc answered. "Before he left, he was the kind of man I thought I wanted to be. Now he's the kind of man I've become."

"Says who?" Cooper took a long pull on his beer.

"Probably Remi at this point. The fact that I can't commit means I hurt her. My fear of abandonment, thanks to dear old Dad, made me overreact to her news. I've messed it all up just like he did."

Damon planted his palms on the bar and leaned forward. "You've made a couple of missteps with a woman. You didn't desert her and your four sons and unborn daughter never to look back."

"Because we don't have kids. But I might desert them if she gave me another chance."

Max scoffed. "You could also shove your finger into a light socket based on the dumb stuff coming out of your mouth. But I hope you won't be that stupid."

"What did Remi say to you to get you so freaked out?" Coop asked him.

"She told me she loved me."

"Can we assume you did not reciprocate the sentiment?" Cooper asked.

"No." Linc shook his head.

"But you *do* love her," Max prompted.

Linc pressed two fingers against the deep ache in his chest. "I do, and it scares the hell out of me. The inheritance changes things. Maybe Wendell Fortune was right to keep it from us. Having this kind of wealth is supposed to make things easier. It was my chance to throw off the mantle of responsibility I'd lived with for many years. I shouldn't have a care in the world."

Max shook his head. "But that hasn't worked because you're a guy who cares about things. Maybe you wanted to be like Dad, Linc. But the rest of us had a better role model. We had you. You took on more responsibility than you should have. Maybe it wasn't always easy, but you made it look natural."

"He's right," Cooper agreed. "About all of it."

Damon pushed a bowl of peanuts toward Linc. "You know Remi doesn't care about your money. She wouldn't make you commit to things you aren't ready for."

"She knows you better than you know yourself," Max offered. "Maybe if you don't have faith in your ability to do right by her, you can rely on her faith for a while."

"You can rely on our faith," Damon added. "Don't let fear or issues Rick Maloney left you with rule the day. That man doesn't deserve power or a role in our lives."

Damon waved to a couple who'd just sat down at the end of the bar. "I need to wait on real customers, but you should take my advice. Bartenders know what we're talking about. We are very wise."

Linc's glance traveled between Max and Cooper.

"I'm not going to admit that Damon is wise," Cooper said with a chuckle.

"But he's right." Max nudged Linc. "The money hasn't changed you. It's given you more to think about—rich guy problems—but you've had trouble adjusting because you're a good guy. You want to do the right thing and make a difference."

"You're more than just a boring, responsible stick-in-the-mud," Cooper confirmed.

Linc blew out a laugh. "That's a comfort."

"You know what I mean," Cooper told him. "You might not want to admit you care. You might want everyone to believe in your overactive sense of duty, but you do care. That doesn't make you weak. It makes you stronger. It's what separates you from the man our dad was. I don't know what's going to happen with you and Remi, but Rick was a coward. He abandoned Mom and us because he was too afraid to man up. If you're looking to emulate Dad, you're doing exactly what he would by letting fear rule the day."

"You aren't him," Max said simply.

Linc swallowed around the ball of emotion lodged in his throat. "I need to go home. I've got some decisions to make."

"Do us all a favor and sleep off this little interlude before making any rash moves," Cooper told him, apparently not the only surprisingly smart guy here tonight.

"When did my younger brothers suddenly get so wise?"

"You taught us." Max clapped him on the shoulder as Linc slipped off the stool. "Let's get out of here."

Linc waved to Damon as he followed Max and Cooper out of the bar, feeling about a hundred pounds lighter than he had when he walked in. Why had he never considered that he had a choice as to whether he wanted to take after Rick Maloney or not?

He had a good life and liked taking care of people. He wanted to take care of Remi.

She'd believed in him before he'd inherited his money, and he wanted to show her that he could be the kind of man who would deserve a place at her side. As he watched his hometown roll by out of the passenger side of his fancy sports car, he understood that he also wanted to be a man who would do more with his grandfather's legacy than blow it on trips and unnecessary purchases.

No one else could determine his purpose. It was his responsibility.

His gaze caught on the shuttered hardware store, which had gone out of business a few years after GreatStore opened. Linc could remember weekend mornings picking out penny candy when he ran errands with his dad.

A fair number of local businesses had closed after GreatStore came to town.

He thought about the difference between his home and Rambling Rose, where his sister lived. Suddenly, an idea came to him. He didn't necessarily want to be a big-time real estate developer like some of his Rambling Rose cousins, but he hoped to add value to his hometown.

More importantly, he wanted to do it in partnership with Remi. He could see his future as clear as the winter sky above him. For the first time in a long time, he smiled, knowing that he would soon be the happiest man in Texas if his plan worked.

Chapter Nineteen

It had been three days since Remi and Linc had ar-
gued in the book section of GreatStore. She had the
whole department dismantled at this point and was
working on new displays of brightly colored phones
and computer cases along with tablets children could
use for both educational and entertainment purposes.

It felt as though pieces of her heart had been
scraped away with every book she packed and doubts
about her choice to stay in Chatelaine continued to
plague her. But this town was her home. She might
have initially returned to support her mom, but now
Remi couldn't see herself living anywhere else. She'd
find a way to recover from her heartbreak and she'd
continue to do her best to be an advocate for reading within the community.

She'd convinced Paul to allow her to keep a few

bestsellers on a shelf near a display of e-readers. They'd included signage reminding customers that, in addition to playing games and scrolling social media on their new devices, they could also read. It seemed straightforward enough to her, but she'd been surprised by the number of people who'd asked for assistance downloading a reading app.

She'd heard from her mother that Linc had gone out of town for a couple of days and wondered if he knew that she'd decided to stay in Chatelaine.

Maybe he didn't want to be that close to her or he'd met a woman someplace else that would help him forget about Remi. She shook her head and refused to believe that he could get over her so quickly.

Their time together had meant something, and not just because they'd been friends for years.

Lincoln Fortune Maloney might not be able to admit he cared about her, but she knew that he had. She wasn't going to sell herself short any longer, even if that meant she'd be nursing a broken heart for the foreseeable future.

"Hey."

She whirled at the sound of Linc's voice behind her. He stood at the end of the aisle like she'd conjured him up with her thoughts.

"How are you?" He ran a hand through his rumpled hair. He wore a wrinkled flannel shirt and baggy jeans, looking tired but so perfect and familiar.

All she wanted to do was rush forward and throw herself into his arms. But she took only one measured step toward him. He'd made his choice, and they both had to live with that. Surely it would get easier to run into him around town. Eventually she'd get over Linc, but for now, she could pretend.

"I'm okay. Keeping busy." She waved a hand toward the shelves. "You know."

"Things look great here," he said, following her gaze. "You have the touch."

Why did he have to say something nice? It would be simpler to harden her heart if he was a jerk. Remi grasped for something that would remind them both of the distance between them. She tipped up her chin. "I'm staying in Chatelaine," she told him, proud that her voice didn't shake.

"I heard that." Something flashed in his gaze but was gone before she could define it. "My mom and yours have struck up quite a friendship."

"It's good to have friends," Remi said quietly. She tried to ignore the tightness in her chest.

"Friends are the best." Linc's throat bobbed as he swallowed, then met her gaze. His eyes were filled with remorse and something else she couldn't name. "You're the best. You're my best friend, Remi."

Tears stung the back of her eyes. She wanted to believe him, but he'd hurt her so badly. "It hasn't felt that way."

"I know, and I'm sorry."

A noise behind him caught her attention, and she noticed that Alana, Alec, Paul and several other of her coworkers were watching once again. Remi wasn't sure whether to laugh or cringe at the thought of having another conversation with Linc in front of an audience.

"Do you want to talk someplace private?" she offered.

He surprised her by shaking his head. "It's better this way." He turned and waved to the growing crowd. "You all heard me muck this up a few days ago, so I want to be sure you hear me try to fix it."

"We're ready, so stop dinking around," Paul told him with a wink. "Get to the good part, Linc."

Remi drew in a shuddery breath as Linc returned his gaze to hers. His green eyes sparkled with emotion. "You are the good part, Remi. You always have been, at least for me."

"Le sigh," Alana called.

"Quiet," Alec told her. "Don't distract him."

Remi pressed her lips together to keep from giggling. "Are you sure you don't want to lose the peanut gallery?"

"Let them heckle me." He took a step toward her, and the heat in his gaze seemed to pull the scattered pieces of her heart back together. "It might have taken me a bit of time to pull my head...to get my head on straight. But it's there now." He cleared his throat. "I love you, Remi Reynolds. You are not only my best friend, but you're also the love of my life. You hold my heart in your hands, and you're the only person I would trust with it."

"Linc." Emotion surged in her chest like a wave

building strength as it rolled toward shore. This man was her solid ground. He always had been.

"I know I haven't treated you the way you deserve, but if you give me another chance, that's going to change. I want to honor and cherish you for as long as you'll put up with me. I can't imagine my life without you in it. You make everything right and good."

"I don't know what to say." She pressed a hand to her pounding heart. "In my wildest dreams I couldn't have imagined this moment." She hadn't imagined that she would ever get the life she'd dreamed of and now that it was happening, she'd lost all ability to think. Her mind was blissfully blank as her heart took over.

"Say you love him back," Alana advised in a sing-song voice. "Duh."

"I love you back," Remi dutifully repeated, tears slipping from her eyes. "But you know that already."

"I thought I'd lost you," Linc admitted as he brushed a thumb along her cheek. "It doesn't matter how much money I have in the bank. Nothing is worth a single penny without you. You give my life purpose. I want to have all my adventures with you, whether they're big or small."

"That's because you secretly love Scrabble," she said with a grin.

"I not so secretly love you," he answered. "I have plans for our future. Please tell me we have a future."

"Linc, I've loved you for so long it's almost embarrassing. I thought I was okay with friendship, but these past few weeks have changed all that. You've changed me. You've made me feel like I'm worth more than I thought. You've helped me believe in myself."

They were standing toe to toe, and he drew his hands up her arms and along her shoulders until he cradled her face. "I love you. I love you. I love you. I know it took me too long to say it, but now I'm going to tell you so often you'll get sick of hearing me."

She beamed. "Somehow I doubt that."

"Kiss her!" the crowd demanded.

Linc leaned in and brushed his lips over hers, eliciting cheers from their friends. "I didn't need them to tell me," he said, his words tickling her mouth.

She wrapped her arms around his neck and kissed him back with all the love inside her. "I love you, Linc."

"There's just one more thing," he said suddenly, pulling back.

He interlaced their fingers and turned. "Hey, Paul. Remi's going to take her lunch break, okay?"

"Take as long as you need."

Linc squeezed Remi's hand. "Can I show you something?"

"Say yes," Alana urged in a stage whisper.

Remi didn't need to be told twice. "Yes."

Linc wasn't sure why he was so nervous as he drove Remi from the GreatStore parking lot toward downtown.

"Going incognito in the truck today?" she asked as she smiled at him. Her smile lit up his heart.

"I've decided to save the Ferrari for weekends with my girl. It's fun and fast, but I have more important dreams to attend to. And those dreams are going to take a more practical set of wheels. I hope you aren't too disappointed. I could always trade in this baby for a newer model."

She snorted out a laugh. "You won't hear me encouraging you to trade in for a newer model, Linc. I like things fine the way they are right now."

He parked at the curb in front of one of the boarded-up storefronts along the town's main drag.

"What are we doing here?" she asked.

He leaned across the console and kissed her. "Making plans."

They got out of the truck and he took her hand. "Do you remember this place?"

She frowned. "The old hardware store? Sure. My dad used to take me and my sisters here with him on weekend mornings."

"Mine, too. Before he left, that is."

"Your dad was stupid," she said simply.

"Yes, but luckily I don't take after him." He drew her closer and nuzzled her neck. She made the sweetest sound in response and he forced himself to focus on what he wanted to say. "I've been thinking about my purpose, Remi."

"You mean outside of making me happy, which you've already accomplished?"

"I hope I'm going to make you even happier. I want to give back to Chatelaine. I'd like to do good in our town. Our home."

"I'd like that, too."

He cleared his throat and stepped away from her, pulling the sign he'd had made from the back of his truck. The block letters had been painted in robin's-egg blue on a background of reclaimed boards that had been joined together.

"What do you think?" he asked as he flipped it to face her.

"Remi's Reads," she read slowly. "I don't understand."

"A bookstore in Chatelaine," he told her. "Right here." He gestured toward the hardware store. "I've already talked to the building's owner. He's willing to give us a great deal on the space."

"Us?" She looked adorably baffled.

"You and me. I want to open a bookstore here in town." He rested the sign against one of the truck's tires and took her hand. "I looked up the store that made you an offer in San Antonio and got some initial ideas about running a successful independent bookstore. This is my future. My purpose. Our purpose if you want it, Remi."

She let out a small sound that sounded somewhere between a yelp and a sob. "You want us to open a bookstore together?"

He nodded. "I want to use my inheritance to do good in this town. Maybe if Wendell Fortune had invested more in this community, he would have understood how special it is. I get that now. You helped me see it. I don't need fancy trips or sports cars. I need to feel like my life has meaning. I want to find that meaning in something we do together. What do you think?"

She launched herself at him, and he wrapped his arms around her. "I think this is the most amazing idea I've ever heard. I already have plans, Linc. For us. For the bookstore. For our future."

"Whatever you want, sweetheart," he said, his heart exploding with love.

"I want you and me together."

"Then your wish is my command." He kissed her again, knowing his future would be everything he could imagine and more with the woman he loved at his side.

* * * * *

Look for the next installment of the new continuity
The Fortunes of Texas: Hitting the Jackpot
Don't miss

Fortune's Dream House
by Nina Crespo

On sale February 2023, wherever Harlequin
books and ebooks are sold.

COMING NEXT MONTH FROM

ⒽHARLEQUIN®
SPECIAL EDITION™

#2959 FORTUNE'S DREAM HOUSE
The Fortunes of Texas: Hitting the Jackpot • by Nina Crespo
For Max Fortune Maloney to get his ranch bid accepted, he has to convince his agent, Eliza Henry, to pretend they're heading for the altar. Eliza needs the deal to advance her career, but she fears jeopardizing her reputation almost as much as she does falling for the sweet-talking cowboy.

#2960 SELLING SANDCASTLE
The McFaddens of Tinsley Cove • by Nancy Robards Thompson
Moving to North Carolina to be a part of a reality real estate show was never in newly divorced Cassie Houston's plans but she needs a fresh start. That fresh start was not going to include romance—still, the sparks flying between her and fellow costar Logan McFadden are impossible to deny. But they both have difficult pasts and sparks might not be enough.

#2961 THE COWBOY'S MISTAKEN IDENTITY
Dawson Family Ranch • by Melissa Senate
While looking for his father, rancher Chase Dawson finds an irate woman. *How could he abandon her and their son?* The problem is, Chase doesn't have a baby. But he does have a twin. Chase vows to right his brother's wrongs and be the man Hannah Calhoun and his nephew need. Can his love break through Hannah's guarded heart?

#2962 THE VALENTINE'S DO-OVER
by Michelle Lindo-Rice
When radio personalities Selena Cartwright and Trent Moon share why they've sworn off love and hate Valentine's Day, the gala celebrating singlehood is born! Planning the event has Trent and Selena seeing, and wanting, each other more than just professionally. As the gala approaches, can they overcome past heartache and possibly discover that Trent + Selena = True Love 4-Ever?

#2963 VALENTINES FOR THE RANCHER
Aspen Creek Bachelors • by Kathy Douglass
Jillian Adams expected Miles Montgomery to propose—she got a breakup speech instead! Now Jillian is back, and their ski resort hometown is heating up! Their kids become inseparable, making it impossible to avoid each other. So when the rancher asks Jillian for forgiveness and a Valentine's Day dance, can she trust him, and her heart, this time?

#2964 WHAT HAPPENS IN THE AIR
Love in the Valley • by Michele Dunaway
After Luke Thornton shattered her heart, Shelby Bien fled town to become a jet-setting photographer. Shelby's shocked to find that single dad Luke's back in New Charles. When they join forces to fly their families' hot-air balloon, it's Shelby's chance at a cover story. And, just maybe, a second chance for the former sweethearts' own story!

YOU CAN FIND MORE INFORMATION ON UPCOMING HARLEQUIN TITLES, FREE EXCERPTS AND MORE AT HARLEQUIN.COM.

HSECNM1222

Get 4 FREE REWARDS!

We'll send you 2 FREE Books plus 2 FREE Mystery Gifts.

FREE Value Over **$20**

Both the **Harlequin® Special Edition** and **Harlequin® Heartwarming™** series feature compelling novels filled with stories of love and strength where the bonds of friendship, family and community unite.

YES! Please send me 2 FREE novels from the Harlequin Special Edition or Harlequin Heartwarming series and my 2 FREE gifts (gifts are worth about $10 retail). After receiving them, if I don't wish to receive any more books, I can return the shipping statement marked "cancel." If I don't cancel, I will receive 6 brand-new Harlequin Special Edition books every month and be billed just $5.49 each in the U.S. or $6.24 each in Canada, a savings of at least 12% off the cover price, or 4 brand-new Harlequin Heartwarming Larger-Print books every month and be billed just $6.24 each in the U.S. or $6.74 each in Canada, a savings of at least 19% off the cover price. It's quite a bargain! Shipping and handling is just 50¢ per book in the U.S. and $1.25 per book in Canada.* I understand that accepting the 2 free books and gifts places me under no obligation to buy anything. I can always return a shipment and cancel at any time by calling the number below. The free books and gifts are mine to keep no matter what I decide.

Choose one: ☐ **Harlequin Special Edition**
(235/335 HDN GRJV)

☐ **Harlequin Heartwarming Larger-Print**
(161/361 HDN GRJV)

Name (please print)

Address   Apt. #

City   State/Province   Zip/Postal Code

Email: Please check this box ☐ if you would like to receive newsletters and promotional emails from Harlequin Enterprises ULC and its affiliates. You can unsubscribe anytime.

Mail to the **Harlequin Reader Service:**
IN U.S.A.: P.O. Box 1341, Buffalo, NY 14240-8531
IN CANADA: P.O. Box 603, Fort Erie, Ontario L2A 5X3

Want to try 2 free books from another series! Call 1-800-873-8635 or visit www.ReaderService.com.

*Terms and prices subject to change without notice. Prices do not include sales taxes, which will be charged (if applicable) based on your state or country of residence. Canadian residents will be charged applicable taxes. Offer not valid in Quebec. This offer is limited to one order per household. Books received may not be as shown. Not valid for current subscribers to the Harlequin Special Edition or Harlequin Heartwarming series. All orders subject to approval. Credit or debit balances in a customer's account(s) may be offset by any other outstanding balance owed by or to the customer. Please allow 4 to 6 weeks for delivery. Offer available while quantities last.

Your Privacy—Your information is being collected by Harlequin Enterprises ULC, operating as Harlequin Reader Service. For a complete summary of the information we collect, how we use this information and to whom it is disclosed, please visit our privacy notice located at corporate.harlequin.com/privacy-notice. From time to time we may also exchange your personal information with reputable third parties. If you wish to opt out of this sharing of your personal information, please visit readerservice.com/consumerchoice or call 1-800-873-8635. **Notice to California Residents**—Under California law, you have specific rights to control and access your data. For more information on these rights and how to exercise them, visit corporate.harlequin.com/california-privacy.

HSEHW22R3

HARLEQUIN
PLUS

Try the best multimedia subscription service for romance readers like you!

Read, Watch and Play.

Experience the easiest way to get the romance content you crave.

Start your **FREE TRIAL** at
<u>www.harlequinplus.com/freetrial</u>.